Cape Hatteras Castaway

by

Sharron Frink

Please enjoy these other riveting

novels

by Sharron Frink:

more Southern stories:

- Buffalo City Moonshine Murders
- Longview Legacy
- Saving Madison
- Bertie
- Prisoner of Experience

…and if you like a little clean, thought-provoking futuristic fiction:

- Family Protection Act
- Family Protection Act II – The Seed of Life
- Family Protection Act III – The Unknown Asset

all available as both e-books and paperbacks at

amazon.com

Grateful thanks to my First Readers – my husband Rand and my daughter in law Alicia – for their editing skills and their patience, putting up with an author in the family. And a special kind of appreciation goes out to the very best editor that money cannot buy – Penny Jeavons.

Thanks as well to my growing family of readers and supporters who appreciate reading an entertaining "clean" story.

Prologue

THE YEAR OF OUR LORD 1886

HATTERAS ISLAND, NORTH CAROLINA

Sarah was dragged along – kicking, coughing and screaming – through the turbulent, icy cold water by strong arms that refused to let her go. The harsh wind battered her wet face and stung her eyes as she tried to open them. Only vague shadows could be discerned in this - the blackest night she had ever known! She made out shadows of a man who now had her by the arms, leaning over her, wrestling relentlessly against the grip of the sea for possession of her body. It was a battle between the man and the water, and it wasn't over yet.

In her blind panic, the young woman struggled; all she wanted to do was collapse, but those same unyielding arms kept pulling her through the water until her feet touched sand. Finally, she was wrenched from the grasp of the sea and felt the cold winds pressing her soggy clothing against her body. She had felt numb in the cold water, but now the wind drove the cold into her like tiny knives, cutting into every inch of her exposed flesh. She moaned and struggled.

A second set of arms grabbed hold of her and she felt herself being dragged further ashore onto the sandy beach. The background noise of howling wind and crashing waves made it difficult to hear, but she thought that she made out someone yelling. Not the screaming voices of the dying that she'd just heard, but new ones…if they were indeed voices.

Salty seawater spewed from her mouth and burned her eyes. "Do ye reckon she's the only one, Josiah?" she heard a man say as she gasped for breath.

"Aye, I do. The only reason I found *her* was because she would not stop screaming!" a deeper voice answered. "No, Erv, don't let's put her down here, we must get her inside where we can get these clothes off of her!"

She felt herself being dragged up and over a sandy hill. The impact of the man's last words finally hit her and she began to struggle and scream again. "Don't hurt me – please don't hurt me!" she begged, coughing out the words as best she could.

The roar of the wind almost drowned out the last thing she heard before she fainted: "Now you have gone and scared her, Josiah, the poor thing thinks we means to do her harm!"

The large man threw her over his shoulder, more seawater poured from her nose, and the young woman lost consciousness.

Awareness came to Sarah slowly; the sound of driving rain on the roof, the smell of a kerosene lamp, the warmth of a fire, the feel of a coarse blanket tightly wrapped around her body – *her naked body*!

She snapped awake suddenly, pulling the rough blanket tightly against her, looking around like a frightened animal for an escape from what surely was the worst night of her young life. She heard the rain beating against the small house she was in and realized that it was still pitch black outside. Wherever she was, it was at least dry and warm; even through her terror she could reason that being inside was better than fleeing outside right now. So she struggled against her fear and managed to stay put. Turning her head, she could only make out a large cluttered room where she'd been laid out in front of the fire. She tried to sit up and began to cough.

"By god, she's awake already, Josiah!"

Josiah rushed over, knelt beside her and moved to support her. "Let's get something warm in her before she catches her death!" he said to Erv. Sarah quickly drew back, spitting up more seawater and coughing when she tried to move.

Josiah spoke softly, "'Tis alright, Lass, no one here will hurt you. We are the ones who dragged you out of that bloody squall and brought you up here to the station house." Erv handed him a cup. "Now take some of this coffee and drink it slow-like," Josiah counseled. "You will feel much better, getting something warm in your gullet... I promise," he said, leaning over her, patting her on the back. With his other hand he moved a cup of something toward her mouth.

She grabbed at it and embraced the cup, feeling the warmth flow up through her freezing fingers and hands into her arms. As her cough subsided, she tasted the bitter brew, but it was as the man had said – the warmth of it in her mouth felt like the best medicine she'd ever had.

"That's a good girl, just take it slow now. You shall be fit as a fiddle in no time," he said as he sat on the floor beside her. The man backed away a bit, giving her the space she needed so as not to feel threatened, but ready to support her if necessary. "My name is Josiah and this here is Erv. We are the surfmen, the ones what pulled you out of the drink. You are safe here, no one will hurt you. I promise you that, Lass."

Sarah looked up into dark blue eyes and focused on the face in front of her. A broad shouldered man in wet clothes, his damp hair clinging to his forehead, was obviously evaluating her condition. Across the room an older man watched her closely. A third fellow sat in the corner, saying nothing but smiling at her.

She tried to speak but could only cough some more.

"Now don't try to speak, Miss, just sip on your coffee 'til you can catch your breath good," the other man said. *What was his name, Erv?* she wondered absentmindedly.

After a few more sips, she tried again to speak. "Wh – wh – where am I? Who are you?... What happened to me?" Her eyes grew large and full of tears as she began to realize the full depth of her desperate situation.

Gently, the man beside her on the floor said, "You are quite safe now, Miss. You are on Hat'tras Island, and it looks like you are the only survivor of a shipwreck. Erv and me pulled you out of the water. We tried to find more survivors, but there wasn't no sign of any. 'Tis a lucky thing that we saw the lamps on your ship before she went down, or nobody would ever have known what happened to you and your lot."

She tried to comprehend those words. *Only survivor? Shipwreck?* "What about Captain Haskins, my friends - the Saltman family – all the others...?" she whispered.

He shook his head. "I am truly sorry, Lass. Perhaps we will find their bodies tomorrow to give 'em a proper Christian burial, but like as not, the sea'll have swallowed 'em up as it has so many others..." Josiah's face took on a pained look as he spoke.

Sarah clasped her cup tighter and tighter until her shoulders began to shake. A strangled sound escaped her lips and she began to wail out, cries like those of an injured animal. She could not even begin to prevent those mournful sounds from pouring out of her – the sobs kept coming and coming, accompanied by a waterfall of tears.

Josiah glanced over at Erv, shrugging his shoulders helplessly. He had no idea what to do with a woman anyway, much less a crying, sobbing mess like this one. His instinct was to reach out and hold her, but he figured she'd probably take that the wrong way. "Now, now, everything is going to be alright, don't you worry, Lass…"   he said weakly, patting her gently on the shoulder.

She raised her head and stared at him; her sobs let up for a moment before she dropped her cup and threw herself at him, collapsing against his chest. Then the wailing continued without letup. He pulled the blanket up between them so as not to have the wetness of his clothing make her even colder, and held her loosely, not knowing what else to do. Eventually she cried herself out, and as she tried to catch her breath in gasps, she looked up at him once more. Her innocent face was begging that none of this be real; his heart was moved with pity. Her eyes rolled back and she went limp in his arms.

"Erv, the girl has passed out cold!" Josiah looked over at his friend, panicking that he now held her limp body. "What do I do with her?"

"Can I help?" the third man asked, standing.

"Yes, Phil, please come and help me… do something!" Josiah begged.

Erv chuckled softly and said, "Just lay her down gentle-like in front of the fire, boys, and put another blanket under her head. We will take her upstairs in a bit. She shall sleep for a long time now, and 'twould be the best thing for her. That poor child has been through more this night than any soul should ever have to bear!" He shook his head sadly, recalling all the times that he had dealt with rescued people. "She will be wanting to talk when she wakes up."

Josiah nodded and grunted his agreement. With easy movements, he and Phil lowered the girl onto the floor, tucking the blankets in tightly around her. Then he sat back on his heels, studying her for a long moment, shaking his head. "I best be gettin' myself out of these wet clothes now…" he said, but made no move to stand. His large hands gently brushed the girl's crusty hair out of her face and behind one ear; her skin was like porcelain – he'd never seen anybody that white in his whole life.

Erv noticed the gentle look on Josiah's face, took a deep breath and exhaled loudly, and shared a glance with Phil, who simply grinned. This situation might could turn into a problem – one Erv definitely did not need. But then, life itself was simply an ongoing series of problems begging for solutions, was it not? And somehow or another, it always seemed to work itself out. He rose to put on more coffee; it was going to be a long night and it was nowhere near over.

PART 1

TO
HATTERAS

Chapter 1

HATTERAS ISLAND, PRESENT DAY

The rolling, crashing waves pounded the seashore as Hannah stood watching. Almost as if keeping time with the waves, the familiar, well-meaning voices rolled and crashed into her mind, relentlessly invading her thoughts as surely as the unstoppable waves overcame the sand.

Hannah pressed her palms against her temples, trying to stop the flow of words she had heard so often lately: "Time heals all wounds" ... "Be grateful for the time you had together" ... "You'll move on and find somebody else, you're young yet..." and the one that had hurt Hannah the most, "God needed another angel." *As if a God of love would deliberately take him away from me and hurt me that way!*

The tears running down her cheeks and the grimace on Hannah's face said it all: the well-meaning platitudes of friends were not only unwelcome; they were not the least bit comforting! She turned her face into the wind and walked on, somehow comforted by the often turbulent seas of the Atlantic Ocean, unyielding and perpetual in their determination to drive themselves against this beach on the Outer Banks of North Carolina.

This place fits my angry mood, she thought. *And I am going to be angry for a long time, too – it just isn't fair! Not fair at all! Why him? Why me? Why us?*

Mark had been dead a little over four months now and Hannah was no closer to coming to terms with her loss than she had been in the painful, emotionally raw first days after that lone policeman had shown up at her door. A terrible, freak car crash caused by a texting teen driver had stolen her husband away from her after only four years of marriage! *And the stupid, distracted kid didn't even get hurt!*

Hannah felt guilty for having that last thought; it wasn't that she wanted the girl to suffer – at least not physically. But she could picture in her mind that same teen, learning nothing from the accident and continuing to put lives in danger. There had been no contact from the girl or her parents, other than through their insurance company. Not that an apology would have made any difference, but that might have pushed Hannah to have more sympathetic feelings toward the girl.

Hannah's marriage had been one of the good ones; they were the best of friends and he understood her. The feeling that life was against her had overwhelmed Hannah at times, and now Mark, her first love, was gone. Only five years before, Hannah's parents had been killed in another car accident. She was an only child; no grandparents or siblings to comfort her and only a handful of distant aunts and uncles. Yes, anger was her close companion these days, lurking just under the surface, waiting to be unleashed on any unsuspecting, well-meaning person!

Will I ever be free of this deep misery? Will I ever be able to face another day and not wallow in this muck of self-pity? Will I ever be...whole again? Hannah knew that if the awful pain would just let up even a little, she could begin to think about a tomorrow, a next week, maybe even a next year...but not now, not yet. She lifted her chin and let the gusting wind blow sand into her face for a few minutes; a different kind of pain was a pleasant change.

Change! That was what she was trying to accomplish, a move that would bring her back to life. That day Mark had not come home it felt as if a large chunk of her had died; a piece of her heart and mind had fled to another place and did not seem to want to come back to the light of day. She exhaled and let out a long, mournful-sounding moan. It felt good to let those feelings out, and on this deserted spot of beach she could let loose whenever she wanted. It was the best therapy that money couldn't buy!

She walked on, trying to put the well-meaning voices out of her mind. If everything went as planned, she was leaving all that behind her now; Ohio and everyone she knew would be a long way away, and she would be glad to have this new scenery. Only one more trip back up to Columbus to get all the details nailed down, and she would be here on the Outer Banks for good. *For good*, she thought to herself, *what a strange saying*. But hopefully it would be good for Hannah!

She studied the seagulls as they flew and dove; Mark especially had loved coming here to Cape Hatteras on their vacations. Whenever they could get away, they'd throw a few things in the car and come down, if only for a long weekend. It had been *their* place, and now it was *hers*...

Her place to be with the sweet memories of the only man she had ever loved. They'd grown up together, dated since high school and gone to the same schools so that they could be near each other. She was a thirty-year-old widow – life wasn't supposed to work like that! They had good jobs, a nice place to live; life was just beginning for them and children would have been in the picture next year if things went according to plan. They were meant to have forty or fifty happy years together before they had to deal with this kind of grief!

Her friends had been right about one thing – she *was* going to move on. But never to leave *him* behind; to leave in the past only the memories of their life together in Ohio; their friends, their favorite places, the home they'd shared – because all of it was too painful a reminder of how happy they had been together. Each day she remained there brought more little stabs in her heart when she spotted a place they'd gone together, something they had shared.

Too many memories! Memories belonged to the past, not the present, and Hannah was determined to make it that way for herself.

Grief was not a place to live, it was a passage.

Coming to these ruggedly beautiful, turbulent and lonely shores was to be a therapeutic time for Hannah, a chance to heal and meditate, to decide the course that the rest of her life would take. Thanks to Mark's ridiculously large life insurance policy, she was a woman of means now, one who could take her time, write her own ticket in life. And her ticket would take her here – to their beloved Outer Banks!

True, their friends and few remaining family members had counseled her against making such a major decision so soon after her loss. They had warned that her loneliness would only be made worse by moving to this isolated area. But as she saw things, it was a move that would free her heart and mind, giving her the space she needed to heal, to continue to grieve until the worst of the pain was past. Someone had told her that it would get better with time; she didn't really believe that was possible, not the way she felt right now - but she hoped that they were right.

She desperately needed to spend time by herself; all her life, Hannah had been an avowed introvert, no apologies made. While some people got their energy from being around others, it was quite the opposite for Hannah. People exhausted her; time spent alone recharged her batteries. Mark had respected this and allowed her time to herself on a regular basis. He understood her, as no one else would ever be able to...

It's funny… she thought, as she poked a piece of a broken seashell out of the sand with her foot. *When someone you love dies, everybody in the world thinks that they know what's best for you… and they're not bashful about sharing it, either.* She shook her head and tried to throw off these negative, ungrateful thoughts in order to focus on the sound of the sea and the sight of the birds floating above the waves.

Yesterday she had signed the contract to buy that small cottage – the one she'd picked out online to stay in on this visit. The feel of the place seemed to fit Hannah, and her spur-of-the-moment decision to buy it had surprised her as much as it did the owner. The old guy had not been thinking of selling, but her generous offer changed his mind, even though the old house had been in his family for generations.

He was a native of the area – what did they call themselves… Bankers, OBX'ers? She smiled, thinking of the look on the old man's face when she quoted him that ridiculously high price for his rental property. It was an old, falling-down place really, not worth putting money into – and she knew it. But she had the money, and if this place was to be her 'money pit,' then so be it; she didn't have to answer to anyone about how she spent her money or lived her life now! In her heart she knew that Mark would have approved, and that was good enough for her.

Hannah was aware that the Outer Banks of North Carolina would be a harsh place to live year-round; it was originally settled by independent minded, self-sufficient types who didn't particularly want or need anybody else around and were perfectly happy in their isolation. Hurricanes, nor'easters, frequent flooding and loneliness were common obstacles that they had to overcome just to live there, and it was little different today than it had been way back then. More roads and bridges these days perhaps, but the wildness of the place – the wind and sand and water – would always be just what it was; no human could ever tame or control it.

The perfect place for me; maybe a hurricane will blow me and my misery away! Hannah thought. Tears began to slide down her cheeks again, but the unrelenting winds dried them up and blew them away as fast as she produced them. She pushed on, determined to walk off some of her anger and grief.

This time next month, I will be settled here and people will leave me alone. They can save their insipid, trite sayings for the next unlucky person who loses someone they love. Hannah lifted her head even higher and walked faster, jamming her hands into the pockets of her shorts and wishing, for all her worth, that she could simply float away on that bubbly white foam as the ocean relentlessly sucked it back in, only to add it to the next crashing wave.

Chapter 2

One month later to the day, Hannah walked into the little cottage, put down her things and looked around. She smiled because she was here, but then... any home felt *so* empty without Mark. Shaking that feeling off, she told herself that he would have wanted her to do whatever it took for her to begin to heal, to move forward. She'd cut all her ties in Ohio and said goodbye to everyone she knew in that area, letting them all know that just because she was living on the beach did not mean that she wanted guests. The few things she decided to keep had been quickly thrown into a small U-Haul trailer, and she'd pointed her car toward North Carolina without looking back.

She offered to buy the cottage furnished; it seemed easier that way, and besides, the place was just perfect it was in her mind as it was. The low ceilings, small rooms and wide wrap-around porch was exactly how she had imagined it to be in her recent dreams. In most of those same dreams though, she had been here with Mark; it had not been only her, alone. His memory would be with her forever.

Hannah looked around, decided where most of the boxes would go and began to unload the trailer. She'd have to run it back up to Kitty Hawk in the next few days, so she needed to get this part finished. Besides, staying busy had been her salvation recently, so she dug in and went to work.

About two-thirds of the way through the job, Hannah took a break, sat on the porch and sipped a cup of her favorite hot tea. The old plank porch wrapped around the east, southern and west sides of the house, giving her a clear view of the marshy Sound as well as the driveway in the front yard facing the tall dunes which held back the Atlantic Ocean. The breezes that constantly blew through here would be a welcome thing in the hot summers to come, she knew.

Now that she was actually here, it occurred to her that she had not given a lot of thought to exactly what she would be doing once she got settled. Simply getting down here had been her focus, and now she was as good as done with that part. She smiled sadly and realized that she would have plenty of time to come up with something.

Hearing an odd, out-of-place noise, she looked around; it seemed to be coming from the north side of the house. She put down her mug, dusted off the front of her jeans and headed down the steps and around the corner. Whatever was making the unusual high-pitched sound was coming from underneath the house. The old place had so many loose blocks in the foundation, it was quite possible that something might have crawled in there and perhaps been trapped.

She listened carefully and determined the spot the noise was coming from. She knelt down on the sand, moved a broken block over a bit and peeked inside, suddenly coming face-to-face with two of the biggest, yellowest eyes she'd ever seen. Hannah drew back, startled, and then realized that whatever the eyes belonged to was not moving. She looked again, her eyes slowly adjusting to the darkness. Something fuzzy was lying on its side – was it a large cat? A dog, maybe? She said softly, "Come here, boy, I won't hurt you."

The animal whimpered so pathetically that she felt her heart clinch, too familiar with suffering herself recently. *So it was a dog!* She continued to speak gently and coaxed the face a little closer. Afraid to reach in, she ran back inside the house and grabbed a piece of sandwich meat out of her cooler. Slowly approaching the hole under the house, she called out sweetly, "Come here, boy – or girl, whatever – come and get a little treat…" She waved the tidbit in front of the opening and heard the dog sniff and whimper some more.

Finally, a comical face popped out, its tongue licking its lips as it eyed the food. She laid the piece down about halfway between the dog and herself and then backed away. Fear battled hunger and weakness until the dog gave in, lunged forward and wolfed down the bite. He turned his head sideways and looked at Hannah, one ear dangling toward the ground. She couldn't help but laugh out loud.

The startled animal began to back away, but Hannah produced yet another piece of the meat and lured him slowly back over, to right in front of her. She fed the dog by hand until all the meat was gone. He began to wag his tail slowly.

"Well, obviously you've been around humans," she said. "Come here, come here," she added, patting her lap. The dog edged closer until they were almost nose to nose. As he moved, she noticed that he limped a little, walking gingerly. She reached out and patted his head and his tail wagged faster. Eventually he came nearer and laid his chin on her leg. She scooped him up in her arms and he resisted only a little before he snuggled up against her chest.

She took a close look at him. He was an armful; he looked like a cross between a large Terrier and a Jack Russell, she guessed, although she was certainly no dog expert. He had a scruffy face, wiry hair and a tight little body with strong legs. He shivered a bit as she held him and she realized how light he was. He must be starving. He may have lain down under the house to die! Tears came to her eyes at the very thought.

Moved with pity, she carried him onto the front porch and put him on the cushion in the porch swing beside her. He looked up gratefully. He waited as she went in to get more meat for him and then practically inhaled it, giving her a big burp when he finished. He looked at her hopefully.

"Sorry, boy, but that's all you need for right now, let me get you some water." She went inside, came back with a small container of water and put it down on the porch. The dog jumped down, obviously in some kind of pain and then slurped up almost all the water. He looked up at her with loving admiration.

She picked him back up and sat down with him in her lap. As she gently examined his legs, she felt no broken bones and he didn't seem to mind her touching him. But when she got to his feet, he whimpered sharply.

"So it's your feet, then... let me take a close look, fella, I won't hurt you, I promise." When she took hold of his front paw he made a little sound but let her continue. She found several stickers in his hairy feet, some of them deeply embedded between his toes. When she felt that she'd removed all of them, she hugged him tightly and set him down on his feet. He tentatively stood up, then walked forward a bit, looking at her as if nothing had ever been wrong, wagging his tail.

Dogs – they don't remember things like that at all, they just go on, she thought. *If only I could get over my own pain so quickly...*

Moving slowly around the porch, the dog seemed much happier and began to jump up and down as if he were attached to a rubber band. *Definitely some Jack Russell there, despite the scruffy-Terrier look.* She laughed and called him over. "Come."

He danced over to her and before she knew it, he had bounced right back into her lap. The food and water had worked its miracles on him and he looked like he was again happy to be alive. He reached up and licked her on the face. Hannah was smitten.

"Well, fella, I've gotta unload the rest of this trailer and you can tag along if you like," she said. "After that, we'll figure out what to do with you."

Sure enough, he stayed at her heels for the entire task, except for a quick break to run over into the grass and relieve himself. Then he was back on the job, 'helping' Hannah. It seemed as though he might have wanted to die under the house, alone and unloved as he was, but her affection and a little food had brought him back to life. By then the sun was heading down toward the Sound, and Hannah had everything, if not in the house, at least on the porch, where it would have to stay until tomorrow. She opened the door and headed inside, followed closely by her little companion.

She tilted her head and looked at him. "So, you think you're an inside dog now, do you?" He wagged his tail agreeably. "Well, you won't be staying inside until you get a good bath, I'll tell you that much right now!" At the sound of the word 'bath' his ears perked up and he looked excited. "Don't tell me that you actually like baths?" He jumped up and down again and barked.

Shaking her head, Hannah took him into the bathroom, plugged up the old claw foot tub and ran about six inches of nice warm water. She picked him up, grabbed the shampoo and started to work. He was a small dog – definitely a male – and absolutely loved to be rubbed with the shampoo. He was painfully thin, his little ribs sticking out like those tall road bumps on the pavement that were put there to slow down speeding drivers. She used an old plastic container to rinse him until she felt he was clean and then she turned him loose and leaned back. "Is that better, boy?"

He wagged his tail and began to shake – and shake – and shake until both the side of the tub and Hannah were dripping water. "I should have seen that coming!" she said, grabbing a towel and mopping her face dry. "Time for me to get a bath now!"

She rubbed him down as best she could with the towel and then turned on the shower and pulled the curtain around the old tub. She undressed and got in. He poked his head up under the shower curtain to watch what was going on. She laughed and shooed him away.

After they were both dry, she sat in front of the fire in her pajamas with him nestled beside her. His fur was a funny kind of patchy grey-black color, as if he were unsure which color suited him better. His ears were totally black, his whiskers black, and his eyes the color of gold. He immediately fell sound asleep.

"You've had a rough time of it lately, you just stay here," she said, rubbing his head tenderly. She made her way into the kitchen, fixed herself a sandwich, grabbed a soda and ate her small dinner. Then she found her way into the bedroom, made the bed, pulled back the covers and fell right into them.

Chapter 3

The next thing she knew, there was a sound as if someone were bouncing a ball in the room. She opened one eye and saw that it was now daylight and was startled by a sudden up-and-down motion beside the bed. It was the dog, doing his bouncing act; when he saw her move, he gave a little bark.

"What the...!" she said, sitting up quickly, and then the whole episode with the dog came back to her. She rubbed her eyes and tried to clear the confusion from her mind. "So, you... you want to go out, do you?" A sharp bark and more enthusiastic bouncing ensued. She stumbled to the back door, opened it and he took off like a little jet.

Maybe he'll go home now that he can walk, she thought, heading back toward the bed. She went to the bathroom, and just as she snuggled up under the still-warm comforter, she heard him scratch at the door. And then again. And again, this time with a little whimper thrown in for effect. Reluctantly she threw back the covers and went to the back door, opened it and he trotted in as if this had been his daily routine all his little life.

"Well, I'm going back to sleep, I'll deal with you later, you little ball of energy!" He looked as though he understood completely, followed her into the bedroom and curled up on the little rug beside the bed. Soon they were both asleep again.

Later that day, Hannah finished bringing everything inside the house; she swept out the little U-Haul and decided that now was as good a time as any to return it to the northern Outer Banks. While out, she would pick up some groceries and a few other necessities to support her new self-sufficient lifestyle.

When she opened the car door to get in, the dog jumped in first, sat down on the passenger seat and gave her a look that clearly said, 'Oh, goody, where are we going?' She petted his head, lifted him gently and then put him back down on the ground, pointing her finger and saying, "No, no! You stay! I have to take a long drive and you can't come!"

The little fellow looked heartbroken, hung his head and walked back to the porch. He waited to make sure that she was serious and then lay down. Hannah was hoping that while she was gone he would wander off and go back home where he belonged.

Six long hours later, she pulled into her driveway. It was dark out, and she had not left the porch light on, but in the beam of the headlights, she could see the little terrier right on the porch where she'd left him. *So much for him running off back home*, she thought. As she unloaded her purchases, the little dog spotted the bag of dog food that she'd bought and began to bounce up and down, barking happily.

"Tomorrow I'm going to have to do something with you for sure," she said to him. "But for tonight you can stay, I guess..." More bouncing and yelping; Hannah pushed her long dark hair behind her ear, rolled her eyes heavenward and asked, "Why me, God?"

The following day Hannah dressed in old jeans, a sweatshirt that said "OBX" on it, pulled her hair up with a clip and then set out on foot to search for the dog's owner. She started with the nearest house, a medium-sized older cottage not unlike the one she now owned. That was the only other home on her street. An old man, gray-haired but still fit-looking, was out working in the yard and she walked up to him with the dog close on her heels. She waved and called out, "Hello!"

He raised up from his gardening, knocked his hat back on his head with the knuckles of his hand and sized her and the dog up. Then he grunted. "You must be the new neighbor," he said unenthusiastically.

"Uh, yes sir, my name is Hannah Stewart and I bought the house from Mr. Midgett. He was planning to move to Florida, I believe…"

"Yep, and he sure didn't let any grass grow under his feet, neither. He put his own house up for sale and took off last week." He looked her up and down. "Where you from, Girlie?"

"Ohio, Mr. uh…, I'm sorry I didn't catch your name…"

"That's 'cause I didn't throw it, you know," he answered, tilting his head a bit and giving her a look that could be interpreted as either a frown or a glare. He sighed heavily. "But I suppose, if you're here to stay, you'll find out sooner or later. Turnbull's the name." He didn't extend his hand.

"It's nice to meet you, Mr. Turnbull," Hannah answered cheerfully, hoping to turn his attitude around.

He made a guttural sound that sounded like he was about to spit. "Did'ya buy the place as a summer cottage?" He was obviously not the type to beat around the bush.

"No, sir, I bought it to live here on a year round basis."

He huffed. "Well, I reckon that's better'n having strangers rent out the place every week and me not knowing nuthin' 'bout em." His tone of voice seemed as though, if that actually *were* a better thing, it wasn't much better. "What brings you down to Hat'tras Island?"

Hannah grinned widely; she always found the way the locals pronounced 'Hatteras' endearing.

"Something funny?" he asked sharply, raising one eyebrow.

"No, Mr. Turnbull, not at all! It's just the way you locals pronounce Hatteras – it always brings a smile to my face."

His expressionless face suddenly took on a fierce look. "Hmmmph! The way us *locals* say it is the *only right way* to pronounce it, you see, Girlie. All you *visitors* make it sound like some kinda Indian name or something, '*HAT-**ER**'-US*.' To those of us *from* here, it's '*Hat'tras,*' and if you plan to stay, you'd best learn how to say it right yourself!" He glared at her.

This meeting was not going the way Hannah had imagined. She assumed that all of the locals would be as friendly as the ones who worked in the stores and attractions they had visited. If Mr. Turnbull was any indication, she wouldn't be making many friends. But that was alright with her, because right now privacy is what she most craved.

Hannah was quickly losing her patience with this old grouch. "Well, I'll try to do that. But I dropped by today to see if you know whose dog this is," she said, nodding to the little scruffy-looking thing at her feet.

The old man rubbed his chin, thinking. "Seen him around lately, but don't know who he belongs to... By the scrawny look of him, he's probably a tourist drop-off. We get a lot of 'em."

Hannah was taken back. "Do you mean that people bring their pets down here and then leave them when they go back home?"

The old man scratched his whiskers and thought. "It's more like this: they bring the critters down with 'em and when it's time to leave, they've lost track of 'em in all the confusion. Usually they spend time lookin' around, but sometimes they just head on home and leave 'em for us to take care of." He shrugged.

"That's heartless!"

He nodded and then gestured toward the beach with his head. "Well, you see, the folks that rent these big old houses on the beach are usually well-to-do. Their kids bring all kinds of fancy games and stuff with 'em, stay inside most of the time, and probably don't get real attached to their animals. At least that's the way I see it... When they take off, they usually leave all the beach stuff they bought out by the road, even if it's in mint condition. More money than sense, I reckon. And then they just buy themselves another dog when they get back home!" He shook his head and harrumphed.

Hannah had quit trying to be nice to this negative old curmudgeon. "You don't think much of the visitors, then, I take it?"

He looked at her sharply. "Nope, I didn't say that. If it wasn't for their money, we'd probably disappear as a town, and we for sure wouldn't have any decent bridges or ferries down this way. The thing that gets to me is that they come down here and act like they own the place, drive like idiots, and wonder why we're not real glad to see 'em!"

"So you just tolerate them, then?" The comment came out sounding a bit more sarcastic than she'd meant it.

He looked straight at her, took off his hat and rubbed the top of his head in frustration, then put the old worn straw hat back on.

"Don't be puttin' words in my mouth, Girlie. You live here long enough, and you'll see just what I'm talking about. We'll discuss this subject the same time *next year* and see how you feel about it – if you're still here, that is!" He raised one eyebrow as though that possibility itself was a long shot.

She bristled but stood straight and stared back at him. "Well – about the dog – you have no idea who he belongs to, then?"

He sized up the two of them once again. "By the looks of it, he belongs to you now." He smirked at her.

She fumed. "Then is there a vet on this island?"

"Yep."

Hannah gave him a few seconds then exhaled loudly. "Would you tell me *where*, please?"

"Down by the Food Lion in Avon. You can't miss it – well most people couldn't, maybe you could..."

"Thank you, Mr. Turnbull, for all the *helpful* information. No doubt we'll be seeing each other from time to time."

"Reckon it can't be helped," he said, turning back to his garden.

"Let's go, boy," Hannah said to the dog. They both turned and walked back down the sandy lane to her house. "What in the world was his problem?" she asked the dog, who gave her a sympathetic look.

Chapter 4

Deciding that this would be a good time to check with the vet – as opposed to dealing with another potentially unfriendly neighbor - Hannah and the dog jumped in the car. They made their way down to the stoplight in Avon. Looking around, she had to drive into the large parking lot to hunt down the vet's office.

"Oh good, here it is, Boy!" she said, parking in front and hopping out, her furry friend on her heels. She picked him up and headed in the door. As soon as he smelled the place, the dog stiffened in her arms. "So, you've been to a vet before, have you?" she said, rubbing his head.

She looked around but saw no one. "Hello? Anyone around?" she called out.

"Hang on, I'm coming!" shouted a deep voice from somewhere in the back.

She waited and finally a dark-haired man turned the corner, wiping his hands on a rag. He stared at her for a long moment, cleared his throat and asked, "What'cha got there?" as he walked over to the dog in her arms.

"Uh… hello, I'm Hannah Stewart, and I just moved here from Ohio."

The man snickered and nodded. "Oh yeah, I've heard you were moving here."

Was there no privacy here? She ignored his terse comment and went on. "This stray turned up just as I moved in, and my nearest neighbor has no idea who he belongs to. I fed him and bathed him last night, but I don't really want a dog. I thought that you might know who he belonged to."

"Well, let's take a look at him, bring him on back," he said, turning and leaving her to follow him.

"And you would be…" she left the question hanging in the air as she tried to catch up.

"The veterinarian that you probably came in here looking for," he answered, laughing softly.

Hannah put the dog up on the exam table that he indicated and then the vet gave him a superficial once-over, muttering as he went, "…neutered male, very thin but seems fairly healthy, probably worms," he said, lifting the dog's lips and examining his teeth. "I'd guess that he's about one and a half to two years old, a mixed-terrier breed but nothing I'm familiar with." He rubbed, squeezed and poked a little more. "Looks like you got yourself a high-class mutt," he said, laughing and rubbing the dog's head. The man looked up and smiled at her. Hannah noticed that he had a single dimple, on the left side of his cheek. He looked to be around forty, give or take.

His warm smile elicited a matching one from Hannah. At least somebody here was kind of friendly…but then she realized what he'd just said! "Wait a minute! Excuse me, but he's not *my* dog, I just found him and thought maybe somebody might have lost him and notified you…"

He shook his head. "Sorry, I've never met this little fella before. He probably got away from some tourists who had to leave – it happens sometimes."

"Yeah, that's what Mr. Turnbull said."

"Turnbull? So you're the one who bought old Midgett's place and the nearest neighbor that you mentioned is Finis Turnbull?" The vet grinned.

"Well, I don't know his first name, but Mr. Turnbull is my neighbor down on Anchor Lane. I just met him, you see…uh, what did you say his first name was?"

"Finis. F-I-N-I-S. That's pronounced *fine'*ess. Like *fine,* fine'-ess. Unusual name, only one I've ever met, for sure. But then Finis is an unusual fellow."

"Unusually unfriendly, that's for sure!" she said, nodding her head. "What kind of name is 'Finis', anyway? Swedish? Dutch?"

He grinned. "Nope. Umm... there's a story behind his name and I'll let him tell it to you if and when he chooses to do so."

"Okay..." she said, sensing that was all she would be getting out of him about *that.* "So there's no way to find out who this dog belongs to?", she asked, rubbing the scruffy little head.

"I can scan him for an ID chip." He grabbed a hand scanner and ran it over the most likely places to find a chip. He shook his head. "No chip. Like I said, he's probably just a high-class mutt, maybe a rescue dog." The vet scratched the dog's head and ears, which set the tail to wagging. "He was probably a real cute puppy, though – I can see why someone would have picked him."

Hannah exhaled heavily. "So what should I do with him, Doctor?"

He looked her over and grinned again. That confounded grin with its accompanying lone dimple was getting on Hannah's nerves.

"You could put up a notice on the bulletin board outside Food Lion, I suppose," he said, turning to wash his hands. "Or you could keep him..." he added over his shoulder.

"I don't have a dog – I mean I don't *want* a dog – I mean I didn't intend to get a dog when I got down here!"

The doctor shrugged as he dried his hands. "You could turn him in to animal control up in Manteo, but it's my understanding that the list of adoption dogs up there is a long one," he said, getting a sad, grim kind of look on his face. "His future would be... very uncertain..." He shook his head slowly.

Hannah's heart hurt. She looked down at the dog, who looked up at her, tilted his head and wagged his tail hopefully, as if on cue. She exhaled heavily. "Well, I suppose I could keep him for a little while and put up a notice and see if anybody claims him..."

The doctor gave her a cockeyed grin this time. "Great idea! Can I do anything else for you while you're here?"

She shook her head. "No, but – you said something about worms? Should I get him some medication?"

He turned and took a small package out of a nearby cabinet and handed it to her. "Just follow the instructions, it won't hurt him and will probably be good for him."

"Thank you, how much do I owe you?" she asked.

He looked at her for a long time, smiled and shook his head. "Nothing at all today. Consider today's visit my contribution to the poor, lonely, abandoned, unloved little fellow's well-being..." He gave the dog a look that hung somewhere between pity and outright tearfulness. "Do you have a name for him yet?"

"Name? No, I... Look, Doctor, thanks very much for what you've done. I'll be on my way and try to find his owner. I appreciate your time."

"It's very big-hearted of you to take responsibility for an abandoned pet like this," he said cheerfully.

"Uh-huh," she said, picking up the happy dog. She needed to get out of here fast; this vet fellow was a born con-man.

The vet winked at the dog as they left. "Come back and see me soon. Welcome to the Outer Banks!"

The scruffy little animal yelped happily as if their whole pitiful 'dog/sympathetic doctor routine' had been meticulously planned, rehearsed and skillfully executed.

Hannah drove home, got out some paper and made up a 'lost dog' notice. She stepped outside, put it on the dash of her car and said to the dog, "Next time I go to town, this goes up on the bulletin board!"

He barked happily and jumped up and down.

Chapter 5

The following day Hannah decided to do a little exploring – not the kind a tourist would do, but the kind a new resident might do. The dog quickly hopped in the car without an invitation and she didn't have the heart to put him out. It was just a drive, after all. He stood up and put his front feet on the door right where the window came down and carefully scanned the monotonous sandy territory as they drove. After a bit, she lowered the window halfway so that he could get a little air.

"That better, fella?" she asked. He yelped and wagged ferociously.

She drove around and checked out several of the businesses in Salvo, Waves, Rodanthe and Avon. Hannah was surprised at the variety of little mom-and-pop businesses she found, as well as several tempting looking restaurants that she'd never seen before. She got a delicious burger to go at a place called *"Burger, Burger!"* and shared it with the dog. By the time they returned to the cottage, she was already feeling more at home here, and getting out of the house had been good for her.

She sat on the porch with some tea and the dog dutifully parked himself at her feet. She looked down and smiled at him. "Well, you're going to need a temporary name anyway. I can't go on calling you 'Here boy,' now can I?" He wagged happily and got a strange look on his face that looked for all the world like a smile!

She laughed and ruffled his fur. "Did you just smile at me?"

He responded by jumping up beside her in the swing and slowly putting his paws up on her arm so that he could lick the side of her face. Then he made the funny face again, this time his lips pulling even farther away from his teeth. She laughed out loud and hugged him.

"Okay, **Smiley** it is, then, but just for the time being until we find your family..."

He licked her again; she took him into her lap. She snuggled with him as she stared out toward the Sound, where the sun was already low in the sky. It was almost fall, the days were getting shorter and the nights longer. But the autumn skies made for some amazing sunsets; she walked toward the Sound to watch for a while with Smiley at her heels. "Stay with me, boy – I mean *Smiley* – and don't run off now. I'll get you a leash, or at least a collar and some rope, tomorrow."

Smiley gave her an insulted look, as if to say, *I am a well-trained dog and do not need any of that*. To prove it, he stayed at her heels.

As the sun began to go down, Hannah sat cross-legged on the sand and was amazed at how this little spot on earth could have such breathtaking sunrises in the morning and then repeat a beautiful performance as the sun went down. Hatteras Island truly was a special, unique place to live!

For the next few days, Hannah stayed at home, putting away and organizing the few things she'd brought with her. The house was beginning to feel like it could someday be *her* home now, and when she hung their wedding picture in the bedroom, she did it without crying, knowing that Mark would have wanted her to try to find a good life, even without him.

The peacefulness and quiet of her days began to have a positive effect on her. She was surprised that she didn't miss the constant phone calls and texts that were a part of normal life in the city. The quiet sounds of nature soaked into her bones and she began to sleep much better at night.

The hole in Hannah's heart was beginning to feel less like a fresh new wound and more like a chronic, deep aching pain that stayed with her all the time. Her life, carefully planned and just really getting started, had been derailed in an instant – by one thoughtless teenager. She felt sorry for herself, but now for the first time, she began to feel pity for the poor girl, who would have to live with the blood of another human being on her hands for the rest of her life.

She shook her head. Maybe someday she'd be willing to write to the kid and give her forgiveness; it had been an accident after all. But for the moment the pain was too fresh, too raw, and the memories too real; if that ever came, it would have to wait until much later.

Early the next afternoon Smiley started barking – watchdog mode – and she ran to the front window to see what was up. The unfriendly neighbor, Mr. Turnbull, was slowly making his way toward her porch. She blew out an aggravated breath but stepped out to greet him. "Hello, Mr. Turnbull, nice day, isn't it?" she asked cheerfully.

He looked up, stern and unimpressed, and came to a stop at the foot of her front steps. "Some might say so; I suppose…"

"Come on up and sit with us for a while. Would you like some lemonade? I just made some," she added. If they were not going to be friendly neighbors, Hannah had decided that it wasn't going to be her fault.

He looked from her to the dog. "So it's 'us' now, is it? You keepin' that mongrel?"

She swallowed hard and put a smile on her face. "Only until I can find his owner."

He lumbered up the steps and plopped himself down in a rocker near the swing. Hannah stepped inside to get the lemonade. When she returned, he was petting Smiley and talking to the dog softly.

"He's very charming, isn't he?" she asked as she set the man's lemonade down on a side table.

"He's a scruffy-lookin' mutt if ever I saw one! Legs too short and a goofy-lookin' face!"

"The vet says he's a Terrier mix of some kind..."

"Well, any fool can see that! Look at that face and those whiskers!" he answered, making an ugly face that somehow didn't quite come across as mean...

Hannah smiled; she was beginning to see beneath the surface. Mr. Turnbull reminded her of her last boss; he tried hard to come off as a grumpy old man but was in reality a teddy bear inside.

"What'd you name him?" he asked.

"Well, he actually smiles when he's happy, so I named him *Smiley*," she said, laughing. "Really, he does smile – I'm not imagining it!"

Mr. Turnbull pulled his head back and looked down at the dog. "No kiddin'? I once had a hound dog that smiled. It was the funniest lookin' thing you ever saw and when he did it, you just had to laugh!" He reached down and said to the dog, "Do you really smile, little fella, or is she just pullin' my leg?" He petted the dog and softly rubbed his ear.

Smiley lived up to his name and gave Mr. Turnbull a big grin. Both of them broke out laughing. "Somehow," he said, "that just looks *wrong* on a dog, don't it? He's got a bit of an overbite, that one, so it's even more comical!"

Hannah nodded. *So this was how it was with Mr. Turnbull...* she had his number now.

"You have any dogs yourself?" she asked casually.

"Nope. All I got now is some lazy good-for-nothin' cats that won't even catch rats unless they're bored to death. They just hang around, leave hair all over the place and cost me money in vet bills! Don't know why I keep on feedin' 'em, ought to just take 'em down the road and drop 'em off somewhere!"

"Cats? I've always loved cats. Well, I look forward to meeting yours. I haven't had a dog since I was a kid, so Smiley is a new thing for me." Hearing his name, the dog turned to her and gave her a look of love.

The old man nodded. "Looks like he already knows his name. Smart dog, I reckon. Good little watchdog, too, and a woman alone needs one of those!"

Hannah stopped to think that over and realized that he could be right. Though the crime rate here was low, if people knew a woman was living alone, it could be dangerous... "Yes, and he's well trained, too. He stays right at my heels when we walk and doesn't bark all the time. But all that bouncing up and down that he does gets a little tedious sometimes."

Mr. Turnbull laughed for the first time, and Hannah found it to be not an unpleasant sound. "That's the Jack Russell Terrier in him. I've known some of 'em to jump straight up, as high as four feet! Darnedest thing you ever saw." He swigged his lemonade and looked around slowly. "You got your work cut out for you, Girlie, this here is a real old place and needs a lot of work done to it."

"What? It looks fine to me!" She grinned and rolled her eyes.

He laughed again. "Yeah, it's all painted up nice, but what's below the paint is maybe a hundred years old, and always needing somethin' done to it."

"Really? The man who sold it to me never mentioned any of that!"

"He wouldn't, now would he?" Turnbull looked at her, realized that she was teasing him, then rolled his eyes and shook his head. "Well, maybe it'll hold up through the winter for you and you can get some work done on it as needed."

"Perhaps when you have a chance you can tell me the family history behind this house, I'd love to know all about it."

He grunted unenthusiastically.

She tried another approach. "And I hope that you'll have a little time to help me see what's needed around here, Mr. Turnbull. I know nothing about these old houses and you've got a lot of experience dealing with them... I could sure use the help of someone who knows so much about this area and these old places..."

He finished his lemonade in one long swig and put it down. "You don't have to sweet talk me, Girlie, I'd help you out anyway. But right now I gotta be goin', got stuff to do, you know. Just wanted to see if you still had the dog..." He stood up, walked down the steps and headed off across the yard.

"Thanks for coming over, Mr. Turnbull, it was good to see you, come again!" she shouted as he quickly covered ground. He waved a hand casually over his shoulder but didn't turn around.

Hannah watched until he had rounded the curve in the sandy driveway. "Okay, Smiley, you know what we've got there? A lonely man who is trying really hard not to like us. So we must be on our best behavior. If he barks at us, we don't bark back, understand?" she said, looking at the dog.

"Yip," he answered and looked in Turnbull's direction.

Chapter 6

One morning Hannah's cell phone rang. It startled her, because she had asked her remaining family and friends to leave her alone, give her some time and assured them that she'd be in touch. Most of them didn't even have her new number.

"Hello?" she answered suspiciously.

"Hannah? Is this Hannah?" a man's voice asked.

"Yes, who is this?" she responded, in her best no-nonsense tone of voice.

"It's Phil Crawford." Long pause. "The vet. You came by my office a while back...?"

"Oh," she said, still a bit confused. "How exactly did you get my number, Doctor Crawford?" she asked defensively.

He laughed. "Well, you put it up on the Food Lion bulletin board, along with the name *Hannah*, and asked for phone calls about the dog... so I assumed that you didn't mind a phone call. But if I'm bothering you..."

"Of course!" she said, embarrassed. "I'm sorry, I had forgotten that I did that, and you're the first person who's called me," she sputtered, trying to backpedal her way out of the awkward situation. "Did you by any chance find his owner...?" she asked, not entirely happy with that prospect.

"Oh, no. I just wanted to check on him and see how he's doing. It's something I do for all my little patients."

"That is very considerate of you. He's fine, in fact he's settling in so comfortably that it's going to be hard to give him back to his family if they call..." she said, suddenly realizing that she'd just voiced feelings that she'd been trying hard not to admit, even to herself.

"Well, if you don't hear from anyone before long, then why not just assume that he's a stray who needs a home. In fact, I think that you two make a good match, Hannah. Did you ever give him a name?"

She laughed. "Yes, 'Smiley' is his name. He actually pulls his lips back from his teeth and grins from time to time! I've never seen anything like it!"

Doctor Crawford laughed as well. "Yes, I've seen that a few times myself. It's the most comical thing – oh, have you seen all the youtube videos of smiling dogs?"

"Really? There are videos? I'll have to check that out," she said, realizing that she was actually enjoying this conversation. "I love the kitty videos on youtube, I can waste hours watching them."

"Oh, yeah, me too. You a fan of Animal Planet?"

"I think that 'The Cat from Hell' is my favorite show!"

"Well, I'm more of a 'It's Me or the Dog' man myself!"

They laughed together. Then silence hung in the air for a long moment.

"Well, just wanted to check in with you, Hannah. If I can do anything for you or Smiley, just let me know, okay?"

"I sure will. Thanks again for calling."

"Nice talking to you, Hannah. Bye."

"Bye."

She clicked off the phone and turned to Smiley, who had been watching her. "That was Dr. Crawford, your vet, he was just checking on you." Smiley wagged his tail as though everything in the universe was as it should be. Hannah made a mental note to take Smiley in soon for a complete physical – if she decided to keep him, that is.

Dr. Phil Crawford walked over to the Food Lion bulletin board and took Hannah's notice down, grinning to himself. He stuffed it in the nearest trash can; after all, he already had her number.

The following day Hannah knocked on Mr. Turnbull's front door, but nobody answered. She knocked again, louder this time. "He's not home, I guess..." she said to Smiley. She turned and walked off the front porch, but stopped. "Maybe he's out back, you think?"

The two of them wheeled around to the back of Mr. Turnbull's house and there he was, standing at the edge of the yard and staring into the rushes that led down to the Sound.

"Mr. Turnbull?" she shouted. He didn't move. "Mr. Turnbull!" she yelled, even louder.

He turned, surprised, and glared at her. "Oh, it's you. What do *you* want?" he asked.

Keeping her former employer in mind, she smiled at him and said, "I need your advice about something. Do you have a minute you could spare me?"

He turned slowly, reluctantly, and began to walk toward her. Whatever he'd been staring at out toward the west was evidently gone.

"Yes?" he asked, giving her an exasperated look.

"I'm so sorry if I disturbed you, but you were the only person I know who could answer this question. My house is a little on the cold side at night. Do you have any advice for me?" she asked, giving him her best innocent smile.

"Cold, huh? Well, I don't doubt that! That place leaks wind like a sieve; usually nobody's there during the cold weather. Midgett always winterized it about this time of year..." He shifted around uneasily on his feet and then said, "Tell you what, I'll come over and give it a look now. Maybe there's something that can be done about it..." They headed toward her place.

"Oh, Mr. Turnbull, you're my hero! I didn't know anyone else to ask, but somehow I knew that you'd know just what to do! Since my husband died, I'm afraid I've been a bit of a mess at times..."

He stopped and looked at her, concerned. "You're a widow at your age?"

"Yes, sir. My husband Mark was killed last spring in an auto accident. I... well... frankly, I moved down here to try to start a new life without him, but it hasn't been easy..." she said, lowering her eyes.

"Well, you must be one stubborn woman to want to start over in this godawful place!" he said sternly. But then he softened and asked, "How long were you two married?"

"Over four years, but we had been sweethearts since childhood. I miss him so much some days..." She hung her head.

He walked over and tentatively patted her shoulder. "It's alright, Girlie, I understand. Me and my missus – Flora was her name; I was just thinking about her – we was married over forty-five years when she passed away. Some days I miss her so bad that I wonder if I can go on..." he said. He stood up straight. "But then, she was a no-nonsense kind of woman and if she ever saw me feelin' sorry for myself, she'd kick my butt good and proper!"

Hannah smiled up at him. "She sounds like a wonderful woman, and I'm sure she was proud of you. I can tell that you're a fine man, and I've only known you for a short time."

He looked away, embarrassed. "Don't let that get around, you hear? Folks around here who know me all think I'm a tough guy that you don't want to mess with..."

Hannah smiled to herself. "I'm sure they do. But that doesn't mean that you're not also a *nice* guy! I'm very glad that we're neighbors, Mr. Turnbull!"

He harrumphed and then said, "Well, let's go take a look at that heating system of yours." He mumbled as they walked, "I *told* that cheapskate Midgett that he needed to upgrade it, but because the place was winterized most years, he didn't see the need. C'mon, let's go check it out."

After a cursory examination of the heating system, Mr. Turnbull declared, "This old thing is on its last legs, but if we baby it along, it might get you through this winter. Then we can see about setting you up with somethin' more efficient when spring comes."

Hannah noticed that it was now 'we' and not 'you.' She gave him her best smile. "Oh, thank you so much, Mr. Turnbull!"

He worked his lips around in a strange way and then said, "Why don't you call me by my first name – we're neighbors after all. It's Finis. My name, I mean. My name is Finis."

"Finis," she said, pronouncing it correctly the first time. "Interesting name..." She left the unanswered question hang in the air.

He looked surprised that she had actually got it right the first time and said, "Well, some day when we have time, Hannah, I'll tell you where the name came from." He fidgeted a bit. "Gotta go now, you keep that thermostat set where it is, and if it that outside unit knocks, you tap it with a hammer right there where I showed you, okay?" He headed down the steps and off toward home.

"Sure, Finis. And thanks again!"

He kept walking, doing the over-the-shoulder sort-of wave once again.

Hannah grinned. "Smiley," she said, "I believe that we have a neighbor who will now also be our friend." The fact that he had called her Hannah instead of *Girlie* had not escaped her notice. Progress was indeed being made.

Chapter 7

As the days shortened and turned colder, Hannah realized that winter on the Outer Banks was certainly no day at the beach. *The wind!* The wind blew cold off the ocean – up your nose, into your ears and all around you until you could swear that the weatherman truly had no idea what he was talking about when it came to the temperature predictions for this place. Weather reports for the area on the internet were a joke; about half the time they were right, and even then not totally accurate.

She'd heard the locals joke about wanting the weatherman's job. That way they could be only half right most of the time and still get a big paycheck. And there was some Weather Channel guy named Jim somebody who was among the most unpopular people who ever came to visit, she'd heard. Something about hurricanes and drama…

Hannah made a trip to Food Lion to take down the notice about Smiley and found it was already gone. She shrugged and told him that if he would be a good dog, she would keep him until the next spring. He looked serious for a moment and then wagged his tail, as if to say 'you got a deal!'

They began to visit Mr. Turnbull a few times a week; Hannah always brought him over a helping of anything good she'd made when she did decide to cook. Soon they were involved in weekly games of Scrabble. He had suggested chess; however, Hannah didn't want to invest the mental energy necessary for that game. But the offer had told her something more about this unusual man.

It wasn't long before Phil Crawford the vet, who turned out to be Finis Turnbull's close friend, began showing up to take part in their Scrabble marathons. Hannah often found herself having such a good time with the two of them that she'd stay later than she had intended. Smiley had made himself at home as well, and Finis' cats tolerated him reluctantly. It was a pleasant feeling to be with two men who didn't threaten her or make her feel uncomfortable around them in any way.

As she got to know Phil Crawford, she learned that he had moved here right out of vet school in Chesapeake, Virginia. He loved to surf and evidently some of the best surfing was to be found in the Outer Banks. So he set himself up and had been here for over ten years now. He was thirty-six and unmarried, but Hannah had picked up references to a woman who had been in his life in some way...

She asked Finis about that woman one day and he looked at her, raised both eyebrows, moved his mouth around in that funny way he had, and said, "That ain't my story to tell you, Hannah. If and when Phil wants to talk to you about it, he will."

For someone who was so free with his opinion about any and everything – and most everybody – Finis certainly kept information about Phil close to his vest. These two must be in cahoots about protecting each other's' secrets, Hannah decided. She found it frustrating, but another reason to respect both of them!

After three months of island life, Hannah was beginning to settle in. Life here seemed easy; she didn't have to go to work every day, could do what she pleased whenever she liked, and had made a few friends. Once a month she would make the drive up to the northern Outer Banks and hit the only shopping to speak of in those parts: Walmart in Southern Shores, Kmart and Belks in Kill Devil Hills, along with her choice of large grocery stores – well, large by Outer Banks standards, anyway. Of course, there were many small shops and she'd been discovering a few of them each time she went north, along with the restaurants she would pick out to try.

She learned that after the tourist season ended, many of the restaurants closed down for the winter, reopening in the spring, around March. Many of those folks were OBX-ers of the new kind, who worked hard during the rushed season and then took a few months off to go somewhere warmer during the coldest part of the year. *Smart people*, Hannah had decided. She'd be planning her future vacations in January or February as well, she decided. The Outer Banks in the winter was not what you'd call inviting. The traffic was much lighter and the grocery stores less crowded, but she was still adjusting to the cold, windy weather.

As the weather turned, their daily walks became shorter. The fierce winds, especially the ones out of the northeast, would often spray them with either sand or ocean spray when they walked on the beach side. She bundled up until nothing was exposed; they kept their daily walks going, but all in all, she began to feel a bit of cabin fever.

There would be beautiful days, though, even in January. The sun would shine so brightly that you'd swear it must be seventy degrees outside, and you enjoyed that fantasy until you stuck your head out of the door. By the time February rolled around and it had snowed twice (in addition to her water pipes freezing up once), Hannah was getting a serious case of island fever – or cabin fever – or whatever you call it when you've been cooped up inside with no particular place to go for days and days on end.

So she read. And she read some more. The local library had a good supply of books about the history of the area, and she found it fascinating to learn about the original Indians who'd lived here, the European settlers, the shipwrecks, the scavengers, the pirates and the airplane inventors who had built life here on this ribbon of sand. Even though she'd never been a big history buff, learning all this was like slowly peeling back the wrapping on a large gift, then happily discovering boxes inside boxes. Her many discussions with Finis and Phil gave her even more in-depth details, and she was finding herself slowly falling in love with the Outer Banks.

At first, her interest was in the story of the Lighthouses, the Keepers and the families who had lived there, manning them – what a fascinating history of hardy people, sturdy lighthouses and even a lightship they had! Hannah came to understand that the Outer Banks section of the Atlantic Ocean was especially treacherous to ships and so many had gone down in the nearby waters that it had become known as 'The Graveyard of the Atlantic.'

Then she stumbled upon the history of the Life Saving Service and was hooked; other than that brief visit a few years back, the stories and accomplishments of these stations and the brave surfmen that manned them was something Hannah had known very little about. How surprising that their tales of bravery were not better known! There should be movies about this!

She and Mark had toured the local Life Saving Station at Chicamacomico one year during a visit. It was the only lifesaving museum on the East Coast that performed the drills that the old surfmen had done. She'd watched as the volunteer Coast Guard men had fired off the old cannon, sending the long rope out to a target up to six hundred yards away. Then they would put someone in a contraption called a 'Breeches Buoy' and haul them to what would have been the safety of the beach. It was most impressive.

But the last year had been so full of sorrow and so much had happened to Hannah that she had given the lifesavers little thought until now. Lately she had been reading more and more about these rough men who manned the Outer Banks Life Saving Stations that had been on the island in the early days. What an amazing effort had been made by all of them! Of the 178,141 lives in peril, 177,286 had been saved, over 90%, during their forty-four years of operation. The monumental effort that had gone into their training alone was incredibly impressive; their valiant effort to save lives had been almost superhuman at times! She began to dig deeper into the subject, fascinated by everything she read.

Finis had told her some old stories that he had heard about the surfmen as well. His great-grandfather had been the Keeper on one of the nearby stations, he'd told her, so his family heritage was tied up with them. She'd make it a point to ask him to tell her more the next time she saw him.

Chapter 8

On a particularly cold day in February – one that featured frigid wind chills and threatened snow – Hannah put her book down. She was tired of reading, she wanted to *do something*. But in the Outer Banks, when it's that cold, you have to get creative. No malls, not much shopping, very few museums open, not a lot of neighbors to visit with…

She bounced up out of her comfortable reading chair and said to Smiley, "I've had it, Boy. I need something to do! I know, let's clean out some closets!"

Smiley looked confused but he followed her into the downstairs bedroom. He was happy with the part about doing something but didn't understand exactly how moving into another room fit into that picture. Hannah opened the small closet door and realized that she had organized things all around the house quite well as she had moved in; there wasn't really anything that needed cleaning out or organizing. She sighed, closed the door and looked around. *Rearrange the furniture maybe?*

No, she didn't really want to get into that right now. She liked things the way she had them, at least for now. *Should she bake something?* Nothing sounded good and cooking wasn't tons of fun for her anyway. So she wandered around the house slowly, looking for an activity – anything – to let her move around a little and do something different.

She spotted the pull-down string in the second floor hall that allowed access to the attic. The former owner had told her that nothing was up there, and she had just assumed that it was a big, cold empty place. But on this particular day, Hannah was desperate for something to do. The rain was falling as sleet, the day was dark and gray, and the wind howled as it blew past the house. She was excessively tired of reading, and even the animal videos on youtube couldn't hold her attention. So, in desperation, she pulled down the stairs to the old attic, folded out the ladder and tentatively made her way up there.

The attic was cold. She went back down the creaky stairs for another sweater and then started again. She could see her breath up there, and the cobwebs were everywhere. *When spring comes*, she determined, *I'll definitely be up here with a broom and some bug spray!* There was one single window, but it was so dirty that the little bit of daylight outside was having a hard time finding its way in.

As she pressed on, bending over to avoid hitting her head as she knocked cobwebs out of the way with her hands, she eventually found the single light bulb hanging from the middle of the ceiling, where she could even stand up straight. Finally, after blundering around, she figured out that you had to manually push the button above the bulb side-to-side to get it to come on. When its few watts finally lit up, she felt triumphant. But when she looked around, her glee changed to disappointment.

Oh, sure, nothing up here! Just a bunch of old junk, she thought. As she looked around, she saw several broken chairs, pieces of an old highchair and other miscellaneous detritus that was obviously cast off from years gone by. Nothing looked particularly interesting and she huffed, feeling that this venture was turning out to be more speculation than actual discovery – and certainly no treasure hunt. When Mr. Midgett had said there was nothing up there, he was referring to the value of it, not the quantity, she decided. This would definitely require some trips to the dump, wherever that was. So she decided to leave this mess just as it was and save this project for a warm spring day.

As she moved back toward the stairs, she spotted over in a dark corner something that looked like – was it a chest of sorts? She backtracked and moved over in that direction. Sure enough, under a few pieces of broken odds and ends, she spotted a rounded-top small chest, about two feet long and eighteen inches high. She moved the accumulated junk from on top of it and saw that it was indeed an old wooden chest, something like a pirate's treasure chest! It looked intact as well. But up here it was cold and there was simply not enough light or room to explore its contents.

Picking the antique up, she realized that it was substantial, but not unmanageably heavy. She lugged it over to the stairs, hoisted it up in her arms and made her way back down the shaky ladder to the main floor. She returned the fold-out stairs to their place and spoke to Smiley, who had been waiting patiently for her after discovering that he was no ladder climber and couldn't jump high enough to be with her up in that big dark hole.

At least she had something to divert her from the bad weather. She hauled her find back down to the first floor, put it carefully on the coffee table in the small living room and stared at it. It was obviously very old, that much was for sure. It looked battered and worn and much the worse for its many years of wear. Between the pieces of wood, the cracks were filled up with black gunk, many years of dirt and who-knew-what else. The old brass hinges now looked brownish-green and the wide leather straps were cracked and deteriorating.

Hannah moved her hands slowly over the outside of the chest, brushing off some of the surface dust. Her mind ran away, thinking of the possibilities of how it may have come to be up in her attic and what it might contain. She knew that the Outer Banks was called 'the Graveyard of the Atlantic' because of the hundreds of shipwrecks that had happened in its turbulent waters over the years. Could it be an old pirate chest? Blackbeard had hung out around here, maybe it was his!

Smiley walked over and sniffed it. He looked at her and tilted his head. Obviously it wasn't something he was familiar with, either. She scooted the table over near the sofa, sat down and reached for the clasp on the front; she found that it was closed but not locked and even though it looked like it hadn't been touched in many years, it came open easily. Lifting the lid, she noticed a still intact rusty chain (one that kept the top from falling backwards), so she propped it open and looked inside, feeling excited.

The old silk lining had rotted away in most places, but the chest was still sturdy. On top, she found two items of worn, embroidered linens, some ragged books, a few old baby things; then she dug a little deeper and shuffled though what generally appeared to be various old (but not ancient) things that had at some time belonged to members of a family and held special meaning to them.

This is so sweet, she thought. It *was* a treasure chest, full of treasured family memories! Her own thoughts turned to memories of her parents and Mark, but she immediately drove those sad thoughts from her head and plowed further into the contents of the chest.

A large yellowed envelope held several photos. She slowly flipped through them. Smiley continued to sniff each thing she laid down as if to say that he was checking the safety of it for her. The top pictures looked to be from the 1940's and 1950's, judging by the cars the men stood in front of (*what was it about men that made them want to be photographed with their cars?* she wondered). A bunch of barefoot kids and an old lady in a rocker, some young girl who had been very pretty then but was no doubt dead by now. The backgrounds looked familiar so the photos were probably taken nearby, judging by the sand and the various bushes and trees.

Deeper into the pile, the photos got older, more staged, as if a professional photographer had come along and told these locals to 'line up in front of the barn' for a family picture, and despite being dirty and bedraggled, they all showed up. *Probably taken around the time of the depression*, she decided. Below that were a few even older pictures, perhaps tintypes, now an aged sepia tone. These looked old for sure, maybe from around the turn of the last century, around 1900. The old fashioned hats, dark clothing and the stern looks stared back at her as she examined them.

One family looked particularly interesting; she paused to study their photo. A tall man in a round cap and some kind of uniform sat stiffly in a chair, a small child on his lap and four other children of various ages surrounding him. Behind the man's chair stood a petite blond woman whose curly hair was put up in an Edwardian hairstyle, reminding Hannah of the 'Gibson Girl' pompadour with a bun in the back. The woman's right hand sat daintily on her husband's shoulder. Behind them was a rattan screen, draped with some tapestry and accented by strategically placed ferns on white pedestals.

The man and woman were obviously trying not to smile – as the photographers of that day had sternly instructed – but they nonetheless looked quite happy around their eyes. The children were all adorable and obviously couldn't stop smiling. It felt good to see such a happy family portrait! On the back it simply said, "1901" with no further information. She smiled, put it down and went through the rest of the stack.

Beneath the photographs she found a few more old documents. She scanned them and put these aside, hoping that they would provide some useful information on the history of her house. On the very bottom of the chest, she found a bag made from heavy red velvet. She opened it and found at the top one pair of very old baby shoes.

Also inside the bag Hannah found a piece of water stained muslin, which seemed to be wrapped around something in order to protect it. Carefully unwinding the material, she found an old leather-bound book of some kind. She lifted it carefully, sensing that it was fragile and might actually fall apart if handled roughly. She figured it was an old family Bible, but it seemed a bit small for that. After unwrapping it, she opened the cover and saw a drawing of an old beach house of some kind, a boat and some other equipment scattered about the yard.

Even though it was aged by time and the pencil lines blurred as if they had been repeatedly rubbed, it was a lovely drawing. The artist had captured the feeling of the place: something important was here, beyond just the buildings and equipment. The wind seemed to be whipping the grasses around, a familiar scene to Hannah by now. You could sense that a storm was brewing and it was going to be a bad one. But something about the stability of this place lent a feeling of safety and security to the ominous scene.

Her hands trembled as she turned the brittle page. The two handwritten entries on the first page were dated – October 27, 1886, and November 3, 1886. The next few entries were dated over the following weeks – Hannah had found someone's personal diary! The script was fanciful, all curlicues and loops; it appeared to be a lady's handwriting.

Hannah closed it quickly and sat back on the sofa, carefully holding the thick, tattered book to her chest. *Should she? Would it be a terrible personal intrusion to read the thoughts of someone who had lived over a hundred years ago?* She gently skimmed her fingers over the cover, feeling the coarse texture of the leather. *If it had been her own diary, would she have wanted someone else to read it?*

After some thought, she came to the conclusion that the person who owned it had been dead for a very long time; if they or their descendants had not wanted this journal to be read, they would have either destroyed it or handed it down to some family member who would have protected it. So Hannah decided that she must have discovered something which had been left for someone like her to find; at least that was the way she saw it. Her brief inner battle over, she decided to open it again.

The very first sentence took her breath away. "It was on the 20th day of October in the year of our Lord 1886 – one week ago today - that I was shipwrecked and found myself alone on this wretched island…"

PART 2

THE
CASTAWAY

OCTOBER, 1886

NEAR CAPE HATTERAS, NORTH CAROLINA

Chapter 9

Sarah became aware of her surroundings slowly: she lay on a small bed under covers, feeling a scratchy sweater against her bare skin and then realizing that she was also wearing some kind of... men's pants. Opening her eyes, she saw through a dirty window that it was daylight out and the sun seemed to be shining.

She began to tremble as words and images flooded into her mind. *Shipwrecked! Her ship had gone down and she had been saved by... some men? And she was the only survivor!* It all came rushing back: the sounds of the ship cracking, the wild screams, the terror, the wet, the cold, the men dragging her here and wrapping her up... The awful memories began to surface and she thought of all the good people aboard the ship who had died. Pushing that grief aside for now, she needed to know, to find out where she was and what was going to happen to her.

She sat up and noticed immediately how dry her mouth was. *Water, I need water*, she thought, moving her legs to the edge of the bed. She threw them over the edge and tried to stand; her bare feet touched the rough wooden floor boards. Dizziness made her sway, but she caught herself on the metal headboard of the small bed. She closed her eyes and sat back down, trying to adjust; she was weak, very weak, and more tired than she'd ever felt before. Her body ached all over. She looked around and saw only other small beds, but no drinking water.

Standing once more slowly, she steadied herself and moved toward the door of the small room, hitching up the loose pants with one hand. As she turned the door handle and opened it, some of the memories of the night before began to come into focus in her mind. She made her way down the narrow staircase, opened another door, walked into the large downstairs room and looked around. A short, stocky older man was standing over the cook stove, stirring something. He turned when he heard her shuffling footsteps.

"And a good morning to you, young lady! You are truly one lucky lass; do you know that?" he said cheerfully, giving her a kind smile.

He looked familiar, and his voice was a comforting sound. She made her way to a chair and sat down heavily, rubbing her face and feeling the mess that was her long, matted hair. "I am lucky, Sir? Truly?"

The man came over to her, holding a cup of coffee out. She took it gratefully and began to sip the strong black brew. She coughed a bit but swallowed it anyway. "Thank you, sir. My mouth was so dry..."

He returned quickly, bringing her a cup of water, which she drank down in one long gulp and then held out the mug for more. He refilled it for her and she took another drink. She looked up at him, and he sat down near her.

"Sir, I have so many questions that I do not know where to begin, but I beg you: please tell me what has happened to me!" She gave him a plaintive look.

He reached over and patted her arm gently. "It is going to be fine, Miss, don't you be worrying now. You are alive and God is to be praised for that. You are on Hat'tras Island, safe and sound!"

"What island?" she said, giving him a confused look.

"Hat'tras Island, my dear, along the Outer Banks on the coast of North Carolina. Your schooner went down, all aboard lost except for you, I am sorry to say. Myself and my partner Josiah fished you out just in time; you had swallowed so much sea water that you surely could not have lasted much longer! We brought you here, dried you off and took care of you. That was... day before yesterday; you fully slept the last day away."

Her eyes grew large and the fear and pain returned. She hugged herself and rubbed her arms, staring straight ahead.

His scratchy voice softened. "Now, now, do not be fearful. You are alive. You are young. You have your whole life ahead of you. That wreck was the fault of no man. The waters here are deadly treacherous, and yours was just one of too many ships that have gone down. I am sad to say that the seabed out there is scattered about with the remains of unlucky ships. The squall that came upon your ship all of a sudden was more than many a worthy sea captain could have managed."

"Captain Haskins is dead?" she whispered. "All the passengers and crew are... gone?"

He nodded and then shook his head slowly. "Tis a terrible thing, to be sure. No doubt the crew were all fine seamen, and did their best. But the ocean here is at times like a wild beast that cannot be tamed by mere men; 'tis fierce and uncontrollable. Some days the likes of us do manage to save a few people and that is why they put us here. We are the surfmen who man the Life Saving Stations along the coast. My name is Erv Brophy, Station Keeper, and this is the Little Kinnakeet Station. But you must call me Erv! What is your name, dear child?"

She swallowed hard. It all seemed unreal, and too much to take in. "Sarah...Sarah Fletcher."

"And where be ye headed on the ship what was lost, Miss Fletcher?"

She thought hard, trying to gather the information he needed from her fuzzy memory. "We came from Baltimore harbor, and were on our way to Charleston, South Carolina. I was traveling with a family that I know who is – was – going into a business partnership with a man who has a large cotton plantation near Charleston that somehow survived the war. They offered me a home and work. They said that since the slaves have all been set free help is needed now in the few working plantations that the war did not destroy."

Erv scrunched up his weathered face. "Do ye have a family of your own, then, child?"

She shook her head sadly. "I did. But they were all killed: my father when I was but a babe, and then my mother died over two years ago now. She had been working for the Saltman family as long as I can remember, and I also worked for them as I grew older. I have no other family, so I agreed to accompany them on their move to South Carolina. Mrs. Saltman has been like a mother to me since my own mother passed away…" Big tears formed in her eyes. "She is gone? They are all gone? The four children, too? And the two older boys as well?"

He nodded. "I am afraid so, Lass. We searched the beach all the day yesterday and buried the few bodies we found. Men we found, no women or children… No doubt they were washed out and now sleep in the arms of the sea…"

Sarah's tears fell. "Those poor children! All the innocent people who died!" She looked up at him as a realization of her circumstances hit her. "What am I to do, where am I to go?" she cried. "I have no one, no one!"

He patted her arm tenderly. "How old are you now, Lass?" he asked, trying to divert her tears.

She whimpered and wiped her eyes with the back of her hand. "I was just turned eighteen the day before the ship left Baltimore." She looked up at him. "*Why was I spared, sir? Why –* when all of those other good people perished – *was I alone spared*? It makes no sense at all!" More tears rolled down her cheeks as she looked to him for a reply to her unanswerable question.

Erv had wearied of trying to answer that same question time after time for distraught survivors. "I know not, dear girl. 'Tis the will of God, some say… but the way I look at it, things just happen for no reason at all sometimes – at least none that mere man can see. I have heard the preachers explain it away many times, but in my mind no God of love would kill innocent people to make more angels in heaven. Seems He would have enough of 'em up there already, and want to let us live out our lives in peace down here."

He shook his head and noticed that his answer had given the girl no comfort at all. "But I am a stupid old man, they tell me, and you really cannot be believing everything I say!" Erv noticed that she was a very fair young woman, despite her ragged appearance.

She smiled shyly for the first time. "You seem a rightly smart man to me, Mr. uh…Erv. And I am grateful beyond words to you for saving my life!"

"T'was not me that pulled you out, Miss Sarah Fletcher. T'was Josiah, my fellow surfman, who heard your screams and dove into that witch's brew of an ocean to save you! He and our third man, Phillip, both be out on the sand now, searching for more bodies. Our job is to patrol a long stretch of the beach hereabouts, and be ready to help when we are needed. The men shall be along to eat a meal soon. Goodness! I almost forgot that I was cooking!" He jumped up and ran over to the stove, mumbling something about burnt beans.

Sarah wrapped her hands around her warm cup and stared out the window. Glorious sunshine poured through from a cloudless blue sky. *How could such a horrible night be followed by days so lovely as this one?* She shook her head and sat quietly, mulling over all that Erv had told her.

A few minutes later she heard the door slam and almost jumped out of her seat. She turned to see a tall dark man coming in, taking off his hat and coat, hanging them by the door.

"Mind you, take off those boots, too, Josiah," Erv called out loudly as he continued to cook.

"Do I not always, Captain?" Josiah asked, laughing.

"And do I not always remind you? Could be the reason, don't you think, boy?"

Josiah laughed, pulled off his sandy boots and stood up, noticing Sarah in the chair. "So the sleeper has finally arisen?" he asked with a smile on his face. "We were beginning to worry for you, Lass, you were out for a long time!" He moved toward the table.

"I told him that you were in shock and needed rest, that was all there was to it, but Josiah still fretted over you, checking on you all the time," Erv said as he moved to put food on the table. "He is the protective sort, is our Josiah."

Sarah studied the two men who had rescued her. Erv was an older man, gray hair thinning, barrel-chested and still strong-looking despite his advanced years. Josiah was much younger, taller and stronger; his dark hair hung a little below the collar of his shirt and his smile was gentle below his full mustache. They both seemed good natured and concerned for her welfare, and it made her feel safe somehow.

"Is it just the two – no, you said, three - of you here?" she asked. "I saw several small bunks in the other room upstairs..."

Erv shook his head as he dished out the food. "We are supposed to be six or seven men here in each station during the storm season – but the fall has come and we have had three men who did not come back to sign up this year – and we were shorthanded to begin with. The Lifesaving Service keeps telling us that they will send more men, but this is a lonely job in a lonely place, and many who come are simply not man enough for the life of a surfman. Come here and sit down, Josiah. Such as it is, 'tis ready to eat."

About that time Phil came in, not slamming the door, but closing it carefully.

Erv looked at Josiah. "Now, *that is* the way to do it."

Josiah rolled his eyes, laughed and took the seat near Sarah.

Phil noticed Sarah and nodded, removing his cap and hanging it up. "Good day to you, Miss! Happy I am to see you up and about. How did you fare? Are you injured much?"

Erv nodded with his head as he said, "Miss Sarah Fletcher, this is Surfman Phillip Weatherly. Phil, Miss Fletcher. And you have met Josiah Miller."

Phil moved over in their direction. "You had us a bit frightened, you did, young miss," he said to her in a kind tone of voice. "But you look like you might just make it!" He grinned at her.

She couldn't help but smile back at him. That fellow had a grin that could put the Devil in a good mood! "And I thank you for what you all have done for me, truly I do," she answered shyly.

Phil shook his head. "I was patrolling way up the beach when you washed ashore, 'twas the two of them that saved you. And I am very sorry that we could not save anyone else... the storm was so bad that the ship had already broken apart before I spotted her, and visibility was terrible. It happened north of here, up where I was walking the beach, but the drift of the current had washed you down this way before I got back to alert the others. I made my way down looking for survivors as I went, but they already had you up in the house and by the fire when I come in."

"All of you pull up to the table while this is still hot!" Erv said, slinging dishes down. The three of them shuffled their chairs nearer the table. He passed around plates of beans and biscuits. "T'aint nothing fancy, but it will do the job," he said apologetically.

"It never is fancy, Captain," Josiah said, grabbing his spoon and digging in.

Phil elbowed him. "That never stopped you from eating it though, did it, big fella?"

Their casual camaraderie was comforting to Sarah. "I'm starving but...I am not sure if I can eat..." she said, feeling a bit queasy when she looked at the food.

Josiah cast his dark blue eyes sympathetically in her direction. "Tis perfectly normal, Lass. Try a bite of one of Erv's biscuits and see if that stays down. If it does, maybe a few beans then," he added, pointing with his spoon toward her plate. "I promise that the food will not kill you, no matter what you hear folks say about Erv's cooking!"

Erv rolled his eyes and began eating himself, too hungry to address the insult. They ate peaceably together until finished, and then Erv said, "She has got no family, boys. The schooner was on its way to Charleston. She was traveling with a family who had promised her work once they got there, but the job was with a man she did not know in a place that she has never seen." He looked up and shared a knowing glance with the two other surfmen.

Josiah looked at her and tilted his head. "Tis pleased I am to make your acquaintance, Miss Fletcher, but this is a sad and sorry day for you, is it not? My heart goes out to you. But do not fret, you will land on your feet. Think of how lucky you are to be alive, and try to see this as the beginning of the rest of your life. God must have something special planned for you, so He will take care of you." He nodded and went back to his food.

His impassioned speech brought more tears to her eyes, and upon seeing them he realized that he was indeed ignorant of the right thing to say to women, no matter what the situation might be. Making her cry was the last thing he had wanted to do!

"Where will I go? What will I do?" she whispered. "I have no one..."

Josiah reached over and put his large hand over hers. "I promise you that it will all work out, Lass. Right now let us think of how to get you cleaned up and all of that..."

She blinked, then reached up and touched her hair and lowered her eyes. He realized that by mentioning her bedraggled appearance he had made her feel even worse. *Time to stop talking now, you fool*, he told himself.

Phil said, "A bath is a grand idea! I take one every month whether I need it or not!"

"Oh, you need it, trust me," Josiah added, nodding his head. Phil grinned.

Erv jumped in. "We will heat you some bath water, Miss Sarah, and you can clean yourself up after you eat. You will feel ever so much better after a bath. The clothes you were wearing were torn up badly but are almost dry, I think. Although why women wear so many layers and layers of things is beyond me..." He rolled his eyes heavenward.

She sat up straight. "You... undressed me?" she asked, looking down and realizing that yes, somehow she had been put into the men's clothing she now wore.

Erv waved her concerns away with his hand. "Tis all part of the service that we surfmen are trained to do. I have helped hundreds of people to get dry and warm by taking off their wet clothes and putting them into dry ones. Besides, I am old enough to be your father – or grandfather. You've nothing to fear from me, from any of us, my dear."

Josiah gave him a glance, realizing that Erv had omitted the fact that both of them had done the job. *Better to keep my mouth shut and leave it at that*, he supposed.

"Hundreds of people?" she asked. "That many?"

Josiah laughed. "Well, dozens anyway. The old fellow has a tendency to multiply all his accomplishments when he is the one doing the telling..."

"Now, you do not know what you are speaking of as usual, young man," Erv responded sharply. "The service got started way back after the Great Carolina Hurricane of 1854 tore through the East Coast and killed so many sailors. Began my service as little more than a boy in Cohasset, Massachusetts, I did. Was trained there by one of the first surfmen in this country and 'tis proud I am to say so!" Erv puffed up a little as he spoke.

Sarah smiled again, and this time it was Josiah who noticed her sweet face. Clearing his throat, he said, "So we will be getting that water hot for your bath, Miss Sarah, and you can get all cleaned up. We have some women's clothes that have been salvaged, so you can pick out whatever you want. I will get them down and put them in the bathing room for you, along with the tub. Erv will bring in some warm water and we will be leaving you alone for as long as you require." He stood up and took his plate over to the sink.

"Can I lock the door? There is a door, isn't there?" she asked timidly.

"Yes, young miss, and we would expect you to do so," Erv replied.

Chapter 10

Sarah did feel much better after her bath. The men had thoughtfully left out everything she might need, from soap and towels to a hair comb. Her own clothing was indeed torn and ripped; it would have to be mended before she could wear it again. She dressed in a badly fitting old lady's dress and then carefully worked all the tangles out of her hair. She walked over to the door and opened it a little. "Can I come out now?"

Erv laughed. "Certainly! Please come over to the fire to dry that hair of yours. You certainly have a great deal of it!"

She bent over near the fire and tried to hurry the drying along by running her fingers through her thick, wavy dark blonde hair. After a few minutes, she began to feel it drying. She sat down and continued to run her fingers through, combing and lifting it off her head as she went.

Josiah slammed the door once more as he came in.

"Have I not told you time and again to stop slamming the blasted...er, the door!" Erv shouted at him.

"Sorry, Captain," Josiah said sheepishly, noticing Sarah. "The wind blows so much here that we must put our back into the job to get it closed on most days, Miss. I forget sometimes..."

Erv mumbled something.

Josiah moved over to warm himself by the fire. "You are looking much..." *careful what you say here*, he told himself, "much more refreshed, Miss Sarah."

Erv sputtered something that sounded like a cross between a grunt and a laugh.

"Yes, I do feel better, you were all quite right about that. The saltwater had left a sticky feel on my skin. But I find that I am sore all over and noticed several large dark bruises. What could have happened to me to cause that?"

Erv said, "No doubt your poor body took a pounding from the waves. 'Tis sore you will be for a while, I am sorry to say. Water is heavy and can hit you hard. And all the while you were being tossed about against the debris floating in the water, which probably caused your bruises. Did you grab hold of something, is that how you managed to come in close to shore?"

She thought for a moment. "Yes, I remember holding on tight to something that was near me... and I remember now being pummeled by other things as I fought to keep my head out of the water. You are no doubt right, Mr. Erv, that must have been what saved me. I remember rushing to rescue the children, but I was washed overboard, away from them by a strong wave and then I lost sight of them. It all happened so quickly." She looked as though she might begin to cry again.

"Well, that is all behind you now, Miss Sarah Fletcher, and you appear to be alive and well despite the tragedy," Erv said.

"And I have some news that may pick you up a little," Josiah added. He walked over to a cabinet, opened it and removed a large leather pouch from inside, bringing it over to her. "I found this on the beach and thought perhaps that it might belong to you... do you recognize it?" He held it out for her.

Sarah pulled her mind back from the pain of the past to the reality of the present. "That... that is Mr. Saltman's, I do recognize it!" she gasped, pointing at the satchel but looking afraid to touch it.

Josiah looked at Erv for a long moment. Some kind of unspoken communication occurred between the two of them. "You tell her, Captain."

The older man nodded and thought for a few beats before speaking. "You must understand, Miss Fletcher, that the law of the sea says that in the event that a ship is abandoned and something from the cargo washes up onshore, it belongs to the one who finds it, unless it can be positively identified. And even then, sometimes…"

He shrugged. "Well, the people hereabouts live by what the sea provides them and usually ask no questions. A small chest floated onshore yesterday and we brought it up to the quarters here to examine it. He pointed to the leather satchel and added, "That was inside and we believe that it belongs to you…"

Josiah handed it in her direction.

"A chest? I had no chest; everything I owned was in my valise," she said, shaking her head and holding out her hand to stop them from giving her something that had belonged to the Saltmans.

Erv looked at Josiah and nodded again.

Josiah smiled at her. "Inside the chest we found this leather satchel containing several documents indicating that it belonged to the people you were traveling with – the Saltmans. You mentioned them when we first brought you in, before you went into your long sleep, so we thought that you might have been family."

"No," she said. "They were like family to me, but we were no blood relations. Are the documents important ones?"

Erv answered. "Not that we could tell. Correspondence mostly, outlining the business agreement that you mentioned. Evidently Mr. Saltman had not yet made an investment in the plantation in South Carolina, but was planning to do so if the inspection proved out to his satisfaction. The chest was fairly tight, so it floated well and most of the things inside had little water damage. Tis clearly his property." He looked up at her and then said, "Do you know if the Saltmans have any relatives back in Ohio?"

Sarah thought but then shook her head. "No, in fact that is one reason that they took in my mother and me so many years ago. They were from England I believe, but they hardly ever talked about their past. They said they had come to America on a packet boat as a young couple seeking a new start – a new life."

Erv said, "Saltman sounds like a Jewish name – were they Jews, do you know?"

Sarah looked surprised. "I… I do not believe so; they never said anything about that. They attended the local Presbyterian church once in a great while, but for the most part they were not churchgoing people. Do not misunderstand me – they were good, god-fearing folks who read the Bible to all of us each night before bed and they prayed with us…"

Erv smiled. "Well, I have read that many Jews escaped to America because of severe persecution in Europe, perhaps the Saltmans were among them… Whatever their reasons, we will let them take the secret of their personal history to the grave with them."

Josiah looked at Erv. "Then it is as we agreed with Miss Fletcher and the salvage?" He tilted his head.

Sarah was confused and didn't understand their conversation. "What do you mean?"

Erv nodded and answered his question. "Everything she said has verified it. I believe it to be the right and proper thing to do. So the question of ownership, to my mind at least, is satisfied. Phil, what do you say?"

Phil nodded. "It is of course your decision, Captain, but I do agree with you. Miss Fletcher is due the property because she is the closest thing to surviving kin that the Saltmans had." He nodded happily.

Josiah nodded again and smiled. "So that would make you, Miss Sarah Fletcher, the closest surviving 'relative' of the Saltman family and therefore all the items in the chest – not just these documents – now belong to you. Come outside and take a look, if you are feeling up to it." He indicated that she should follow him outside.

She agreed and the four of them made their way over to a nearby storage shed. Sarah was still weak; she had to walk slowly, with Erv's help. They approached a storage building and Erv unlocked it. Toward the front of the building was a small chest. She pointed to it. "Yes, that belonged to the Saltmans," Sarah said. "I remember those straps because I thought at the time that they were an unusual reddish color."

Erv stood up straight and said in an official tone of voice. "Then – as Keeper in charge of this station, I declare this salvaged chest to be the property of Miss Sarah Fletcher."

Sarah frowned. "I... I do not know, Mr. Erv. Is that the honest thing to do?" She stood back a little from the recovered item.

Erv and Josiah shared a meaningful look.

Josiah said, "Miss Fletcher, it belongs more rightly to you than to anyone who might come along on the beach and claim it, and any man-jack of them would not think twice before doing so, believe me. We are the only officials of any kind hereabouts, and we declare it to be yours." He put his hands on hips in a way that punctuated the decision.

"However..." Erv said, holding up the pointer finger of his right hand, "it would be wisest for you to say nothing to anyone about this. Some of the local folks are pretty touchy about claiming salvage. Many of the shipping companies do not see fit to go to the expense of legally recovering cargo, unless there is a lot of profit in it. Most of the time there is not, so they usually write it off. As you would expect then, the locals simply keep what they find."

"So, if anyone asks, *it is your property*," Josiah added.

"Did anything else wash ashore?" she asked.

Josiah shook his head and lowered his eyes. "Just the few bodies we mentioned and some clothing, a few foodstuffs, other odds and ends. Word got out quickly and the scavengers have already picked that lot over clean. The chest must have been tight enough to float, and it washed up near my feet early the very next morning before any of the locals came hunting." He looked up at her. "I took that as my sign to bring it in."

"And after hearing your story," Erv added, "the three of us decided between ourselves that you were the closest thing to an heir. It is within our purview to do that. So the chest and all that is in it is now yours…"

She bent down and hesitantly ran her hands over the wet wood. "Well, I suppose under the circumstances…" She looked up. "You have looked inside, I assume, since you found all those documents…?"

Josiah nodded. "We had to break the lock to open it, but we did."

"Is there anything else in there that might be of use to me?" she asked.

Erv cleared his throat. "Haul this up to the house, Josiah, and let the lady look through it. She can decide which of its contents she might like to keep."

"Yessir, Captain!" Josiah grinned, nodded, hefted the chest up onto one shoulder and headed toward the station house. Erv offered his arm to Sarah and they followed behind. Phil stayed and locked up, then made his way to join them.

As they walked, Erv turned to Sarah. "You have your whole life ahead of you, Miss Sarah. You can go and be whatever you might choose. In a way, the tragic event that has ended your previous life has offered you the chance for a new beginning. Have you ever thought about what kind of life you might like to have?"

She smiled wistfully. "Not really, Sir; I was a child… so I have never had many choices. I have been grateful for food, shelter, work to keep me busy and good people to care for me. Can a person really ask for any more than that?"

The older man laughed softly. "You are right there, young lady. Life is truly simple when you get right down to it. Living out here," Erv said, waving his hand toward the beach, "helps a person to understand that. 'Tis the life in our days, not the days of our life,' and what we make of that is all that we have to give to the world."

Chapter 11

The sun now high in the sky, the three of them sat out on the wooden benches on the leeward side of the station, enjoying the gentle, cool breezes off the water. Sarah bent down and opened the clasp of the chest. At the top were a few more papers, and she carefully made her way through those, stacking them into two piles, one to keep and another to discard; most she decided to keep in case they would be needed later to settle the estate of those dear people.

"You can read then, Miss Sarah?" Josiah asked.

"Oh, yes, my mother taught me, and I read many of the books in our circulating library in Ohio. Mrs. Saltman taught me how to do my numbers and was teaching me the keeping of the store's books before they decided to sell out." She took a break then and related to them the details of their lives in Ohio:

The Saltmans had recently sold all of their holdings; he had been a successful merchant and his family had worked alongside him in his mercantile. The older boys were being groomed to take over the business. Sarah had helped out wherever she was needed; her mother had cared for the smaller children and done most of the housework, while the rest of the family invested their time and energy to build the family business.

Their decision to move south had been a surprise to her; it had come suddenly and matters had been quickly arranged. The store was sold, along with their house and most of their worldly goods. They were going to start over again and build a new life in the South, which was undergoing Reconstruction.

Sarah had never asked about money; they had been generous with her and provided all of her and her mother's needs. She received a small allowance each week, most of which she saved. *Gone now...* she realized, *at the bottom of the ocean with all the rest of my belongings.* It had not been a lot of money, but it had been the life savings of both Sarah and her mother. She pictured the bills floating away on the water or trapped in her valise at the bottom of the ocean. Either way, the little that she'd had was now lost to her forever. Truly, she was in poverty now, she realized as she told them her story.

She turned her attention back to the trunk and dug deeper; a few family photographs had survived and they looked as though they might be saved. She was glad of that – she didn't want all memory of the Saltman family to disappear along with them. She would keep the photographs and always remember fondly the family and what they had done for her.

Next, she lifted out a small box containing Mrs. Saltman's jewelry. More tears formed, but she brushed them aside. It was everything the woman had owned except for her plain gold wedding ring, which she never took off her finger. It was all good quality, but none of it would be considered very valuable. She would wear it with pride, however, remembering the loving woman who had worn it before. She set the little box aside.

At the very bottom she spotted a red bag, made of thick velvet and secured at the top by a gold cord with tassels on each end. She reached to lift it up and realized that it was extremely heavy. Using both hands, she hoisted it up into her lap and looked from one man to the other.

"Empty it out," Erv said. "And remember that 'tis all yours, everything in the chest." She slowly poured out the contents into her lap. *Gold coins* – so many that it weighed down her skirt and she had to keep her legs together to keep the shiny pile from spilling onto the floor!

Her breath caught in her throat. "No, no, this is not mine! I would not ever have so much money!" Her innocent face formed a frightened question as she looked back and forth between the men.

"This gold was meant to purchase Mr. Saltman's interest in the plantation, I am certain."

"No doubt," Erv said. "But Josiah and I poured over the documents yesterday and there was no written contract of any kind between them. Mr. Saltman refused to commit until he had personally investigated the possibilities. And while it may have been assumed by either party, nothing was ever put in writing. So no official agreement was ever signed and no money changed hands."

"Besides, Lass," Josiah said, "Do you think that fellow in South Carolina has a right to this money? He was no kin of theirs; everything between them was handled as a business transaction. He might *want* the money, but legally he cannot claim even a penny of it. He is no worse off now than he was before, he still has his plantation. True, he has lost a prospective partner, but that could not be helped and was certainly not your fault."

Sarah took several deep breaths. "What shall I do with all of this?" she asked, running her hands through the coins.

"Whatever strikes your fancy, Lass," Josiah said, grinning.

Phil laughed. "I will be happy to help you spend it!" Erv gave him a look and cleared his throat loudly, causing Phil to add, "Of course I am joking with you, Miss Sarah. I am not allowed to keep any salvage owned by a known person..."

"Keep a mind to your future, now, Lass," Erv said, getting a most serious look on his weathered face. "You are a woman alone in the world and you have no home, no profession and no family. You will be needing every bit of this money to provide for yourself until you marry."

"Marry? Me? I... I am too young!" She looked shocked.

Erv smiled. "You may think so my dear, but there is not a healthy young man in this county who would agree with you." He laughed.

She blushed fiercely. "Can I... can I not just stay here with the three of you for a while?"

The men exchanged a look. "Well," Erv began cautiously, "the wreck must be reported, including survivors and salvage; I will get around to taking care of that. And we will not be throwing you out, of that you can be sure. However, you must realize that a young unmarried woman like yourself cannot be living with three crusty bachelors like us – 'twouldn't be proper-like."

Sarah felt more tears forming and a little whimper escaped her pale lips.

"But..." Josiah said quickly, "as Erv said, we will not be throwing you out. We will help you to find a place around here if you want to stay, or make arrangements for you to go back to Ohio or on to South Carolina if you like."

Sarah's large green eyes got even bigger. "South Carolina? I... do not want to go there without the Saltmans!" She shook her head back and forth. Truly frightened now, she looked from one man to the other and whispered, "What should I do? What should I do now?"

Erv took her small hand in his. "Never fear, young lady. God must have a special plan for you, or else you would be lost out there in the water with the rest of them. You take your time to figure it all out and we will help you however we can. We promise."

Sarah wiped her tears, straightened her back and nodded.

Chapter 12

One night after the evening meal Sarah asked the men, "How did this place come to be? I have been so consumed with my own problems that I had not thought until now to ask you that question. Because of you men," she said, waving her hand in their direction, "I am alive – and because of this station! Please tell me, how do you happen to be here – to be doing this?"

Josiah looked to Erv, the more knowledgeable one when it came to the history of the Life Saving Service. Erv's eyes lit up as he scratched his chin, and Sarah knew that he must enjoy telling this story. Phil opened his mouth to speak, but was silenced by a look from Josiah.

Erv said, "Local folks up and down the Atlantic coast handled the rescues in the beginning, of course; those who saw ships in trouble and could help, well they did what they were able. Then the war came along and for four long years we were so wrapped up in killing each other that little attention was given to *saving lives*... 'Twas not until things settled down after the war that folks began to think much about it being the government's job to save people."

"A man by the name of Sumner Kimball worked hard in Washington to draw people's attention to what needed to be done, and in 1874 the Life Saving Service was set up as part of the Revenue Marine Division and they began building these stations. Back in '78 we were formally established as our own division of the United States Department of the Treasury."

He continued, "There was lots of problems to work out, you see; the stations had to be built and manned, the equipment had to be brought in, people had to be trained. I tell you now that training our men is the hardest part. Not many men are willing to put in the time and effort it takes, but those that do make a big difference, as you yourself well know. Our Chief Kimball has no tolerance for laziness or slackers - you got to be serious about this job to make it as a surfman. These seven stations on the Outer Banks were built and within the last ten or so years have already saved many a life in that time. But this is a lonely, hard life and 'tis not for just anyone."

"This station, Little Kinnakeet, was built back in '74 and is one of the first seven built on the Outer Banks. We're about a mile and a half north of the Cape Hatteras lighthouse. We've got the Gull Shoal station as our closest neighbor to our north, then Big Kinnakeet, Cape Hatteras and Creed's Hill stations to our south. The stations are not too far apart here because of the grave danger to ships hereabouts."

Erv was on a roll. "But, me personally? I have been with the service since the early 1870's. Started out up on the coast of Maine after fighting for the Union, and was moved down here when Chief Kimball wanted a man with experience to take over here on this wretched sandbar. You probably don't know this, Miss Sarah, but this here stretch of waters off the Outer Banks is about the most treacherous on the whole East Coast."

"Why is that?" she asked, enjoying his tale.

Josiah said, "This part I can answer. The cold Labrador Current from the north meets up with the warm Gulf Stream current from the south right out there," he said, pointing toward the beach. "The conversion of cold and warm waters causes the sand to shift around constantly, making dangerous sandbars appear and then disappear. That water is said to be some of the most disturbed you will ever see; the currents and riptides are strong as well. All of that makes for dangerous sailing, even under the best of conditions. But throw in a bit of bad weather, and well, you saw how fast things can change..."

Erv nodded. "Many a capable captain has been fooled by those waters; and many a greedy one has tried to shave off a bit of time on his run up north or down south by cuttin' the corner down off

Cape Hatteras. The fortunate ones lived to regret it, the bodies of the fools are still out there."

"Do many ships get into trouble?" she asked.

Erv laughed, but then turned solemn. "Oh, yes, young lady! I wish that I could say different, but I cannot. But, as I said, between the lot of us surfmen up and down the Banks, many who would otherwise have perished have been sent back home safe and sound!" He puffed out his chest a little. "Thanks to us and the Good Lord!"

"Please tell me about some of the people you have saved," she begged. "Have there been many women and children?"

Erv nodded. "Some. Many of the ships we assisted were commercial ships, carrying cargo, with a crew of men. But almost all the ships have a few passengers for one reason or another, and some are simply passenger ships outright. The women who survive those shipwrecks are the tough ones, not the fainting type. And the minute we fish them out of the drink, they turn around and start helping others any way they can. We have not saved too many children; but then there's not been very many of 'em out there on the seas, thank God."

She nodded. "I had no idea that such brave men as you even existed."

Phil lit up. "And t'aint none braver than the men of Little Kinnakeet Station!"

Erv said, "The three of us here are supposed to be seven in number, and hopefully we will be getting the rest of our crew in soon. You are now fit enough to watch us train, if you like, while you are with us. 'Tis truly a site to behold, what we do!"

Josiah laughed. "Well, at first 'tis more of a comedy act, until we get the new men fit for duty. But Erv pushes us pretty hard and it don't take him long to whip us into shape!" He looked over at Phil. "Phil here is as hard a worker as you could ask for, but does tend to be a bit accident prone from time to time, so we all watch out for him..."

Phil looked insulted. "Me? Accidents? Why, I am as fit and hardy as any man!" He pounded his chest with his fist.

Josiah said, "True enough, Phillip. But you do have a way about you of finding trouble if there's any about...that's why Erv has us capsize the boat and practice righting it so often." He turned to Sarah. "Phil here has a tendency to list to one side or another and he's sure enough turned us over a time or two!"

Phil looked sheepish and then grinned. "Just to keep you men sharp, of course!"

Chapter 13

The following few days Sarah busied herself around the station, cooking, cleaning and helping out however she could. The men relished a change in their eating choices and set up a separate sleeping area for her. Days passed quickly as the four of them got along quite well. Erv finally reported the wreck, the name of the ship and its captain, along with its lone survivor and a list of all of the souls aboard that Sarah could recall. The small ship had held only a limited number of passengers; most of its space was filled with cargo headed south. The entire voyage was supposed to take less than a week, even with stops along the way to unload and pick up.

One morning after breakfast, Josiah came to her, holding out a book in his hand. "Uh, Miss Sarah, this is for you, if you would like to have it," he said, quite unsure of himself.

Sarah took it from him. "A book? Are you loaning me something to read, Josiah? That is very thoughtful of you, I do enjoy reading!"

He shook his head. "Well, no, not exactly. This is a leather bound journal that is for... writing things in. My mother gave it to me so that I could record my thoughts and impressions when I got down here, and then I would have stories to tell the family and all of that. But I fear that I am not much of a writer...so I thought perhaps you might like to have it if you enjoy doing that kind of thing..." He sat down beside her.

Sarah smiled and opened it up; inside the soft leather front cover, the first page held a drawing of the Life Saving Station and its outbuildings, a very true likeness. "Did you draw this, Josiah? It is quite good, indeed!" She looked admiringly at him.

He dropped his chin. "Yes, I drew it. But I did not want to fill the book with pictures because my mother had asked for words. So

I got me some other paper to draw on and saved this one for when I had some words. But so far," he added with a grin, "the words are not coming. Then it came to my mind that maybe you could use it if you like to do that kind of thing – girls sometimes do, don't they?" Josiah swallowed hard; he was always saying the wrong thing to Sarah and didn't want to mess this up.

"This is the nicest gift I have ever received..." she whispered. Looking up into his dark blue eyes, she added, "and it means so much, now that I have nothing of my own, to have something so special, a thing just for myself."

Josiah reveled proudly in the feeling that he had made her happy. "'Twas nothing, really, I was not going to use it and..." Josiah decided that he had better stop talking at this point because Sarah seemed well pleased and he didn't want to talk her out of that, which he might just do if he kept on blabbering. "I am truly pleased that you like it. And here is a pencil, a whole one, to go with it," he added, handing her a freshly sharpened, brand new pencil. "Erv's got pen and ink you can use, too."

The look on her face lit up his heart and he felt quite pleased with himself. He watched as she pulled the journal to her chest, hugging it and smiling her beautiful smile. He felt pride wash over him, and a warm feeling settled near his heart.

Sarah began recording the recent events in her new journal, writing in script as small and as beautifully as she could, certain that she would have a lot to write about in the days, months and years to come. She had begun to feel almost like part of the crew. As the cooking duty rotated between the men, each and every one of them was glad to have her help in the kitchen. But Erv had told her that she would need to be making a decision about her future soon. Sarah immediately put it from her mind, deciding to deal with *that* later.

As the men went about their duties and training, the young woman watched. Their lives were far from idle; each day there was plenty to do. Three more men had just arrived and they were all 'green,' as Erv put it, so watching them learn their duties was at times (as Josiah had said) amusing. Each day of the week was set aside for a particular drill, as Kimball had mandated in 'the Blue Book' of station rules. Every day of the week, except Sunday, the surfmen were expected to drill or clean.

On Mondays and Thursdays, for example, the crew practiced with the bulky, hard to handle beach apparatus. The surfmen had to complete the entire procedure of rigging the equipment, including firing the Lyle gun at a practice pole shaped like a ship's mast. Erv pushed them hard on this one; it required both skill and practice. The entire drill was supposed to be completed within five minutes or the man slowing the operation could be dismissed from the Service when the district inspectors came around.

The beach apparatus consisted of the Lyle gun, a large cannon specially built to fire a long line out to a ship in distress. This line, when secured in the rigging of the ship, would allow the surfmen to haul people safely to shore. Learning to aim the Lyle Gun, in all kinds of wind and weather, was a skill few could master. Only Erv and Josiah were up to that job.

On Tuesdays, it was boat practice. They were to launch and land their boats through the surf in all kinds of weather. Sometimes the Keeper would deliberately capsize the boat, as Phil had said, so that the surfmen could learn to right it in an emergency. The rest of the week the men were busied with learning signaling and first aid. Each Saturday the station was cleaned thoroughly. Repetition of each and every action hammered the drill procedures into the crew. A good Keeper knew that the better prepared his men were, the more likely they were to be successful at rescuing others – and also coming back alive themselves.

Josiah was proud to say that Erv was a demanding Keeper; he had woken his men up in the middle of the night and made them launch the boat in total darkness; he waited for the most disturbed weather possible and made them practice their tasks again and again, often unexpectedly. They came back tired, beaten, but each time better able to do their jobs. One black night he flipped the boat, or 'turned turtle' as Josiah had put it, just to make the men learn to flip it back over in the stormy darkness.

During daylight hours in all weather, one surfman was assigned to the lookout platform atop the station to scan the ocean for any sign of a ship in distress. In order to prevent laziness, no seats were kept in the tower. In darkness or foul weather, the men walked their beach patrols. Neighboring stations were placed miles apart, so a man would walk half the distance to a midpoint in each direction, insert his key into a patrol clock to prove he had been there, and then walk back.

Sarah kept herself busy helping with the cooking, laundry and keeping the small group of buildings tidy. She watched the men drill regularly and work hard and admired their dogged determination and the physical limits to which they were pushed.

Being a surfman in the Life Saving Service was the job of not just a man, but a hero.

Chapter 14

Early one morning, everyone was awakened by the sound of the bell. A ship had been sighted, grounded on a sandbar and the weather was turning nasty very quickly. They were all up and dressed in minutes.

Sarah went into the kitchen to begin preparing food and coffee; Erv had gone out to assess the situation. The wind had shifted suddenly and was now coming from the northeast – a bad sign, the men said. They decided to try to use the Lyle Gun to run a line to the stranded ship, but taking the surfboat down to the beach as backup. Straining against the wind, the men dragged the long surfboat up and over the dunes. They hitched the large dray horse to the Lyle Gun, the gun's big wheels carrying the weight over the loose sand down to the somewhat firmer beach. The rain began to fall, and then to pour.

When it was light enough to sight accurately, Erv determined that the Lyle gun and breeches buoy would be the best for this particular rescue. He had the men set the Lyle gun up to aim it. He and Josiah had to calculate the trajectory, the wind speed, the effect of the pouring rain, and all other factors that would affect shooting the projectile attached to the long line out to the sinking ship.

The line had been carefully laid in a box in a particular pattern, so that it would fly easily out of the box and over the water without a snag. Hours had been spent by the men practicing the laying of the line as well, so that if the shot missed and had to be repeated, it would fly as well the second or third time as it had the first.

Erv and Josiah did their best to sight and aim, and the gun was fired. As the men on the shore and on the boat held their breath, the projectile flew out almost the entire length of its six hundred yards. A great gust came, and the line fell just downwind of the ship.

The sounds of the ship beginning to break apart as well as the men aboard screaming could be heard. Erv urged the line to be re-laid as quickly as possible, and the men pulled it back in record time as the Keeper readied the powder and shot. Phil had the task of re-laying the wet line in the box and he worked quickly, so that by the time Erv had readied the shot the last of the line was pulled in.

Sarah completed her kitchen Station chores and wrapped herself tightly in an oil slicker. She made her way down to the beach to watch and see what help she might give. Crashing waves pummeled the ship as well as the beach. Flashbacks of her near-death in those same waters crept into her mind, but she dismissed them. Now was not the time to think of that! The men fought tirelessly as if there were no wind or waves, going about their practiced routine without a hitch.

As they readied their second shot, Erv took a few moments to double-check everything and say a silent prayer. Josiah set the spark to the fuse and they backed away, covering their ears. The fuse fizzled a bit and Erv went to protect it from the rain and wind with his own body. When the shot went off, the force of it knocked him back and the sound temporarily deafened him.

As the line flew through the air, Sarah prayed. This might be the last chance the men aboard that ship would have, as the waves were now violent and high enough to make launching the surfboat all but impossible. This time the line flew true and straight and landed in the ship's rigging, where it was quickly secured by the crew of the boat.

The surfmen attached the breeches buoy, a lifesaving ring with short pants attached, to a tow line and used the pulleys to run it out to the dying ship. The first man was loaded and the men on both ends began to run the line back as quickly as possible. The man hanging in the breeches buoy looked so small out there over the crashing waves, Sarah thought. A few times the waves reached high enough to drench him, but he held tight and eventually reached the shore.

Erv and his men let out a mighty shout that could be heard over the roar of the sea – they had saved at least one person this day! Sarah's heart swelled with pride. One by one, the crew of the ship were brought safely to land as the ship creaked and groaned and shifted. The tenth man to come ashore was the captain of the ship, a large man who immediately fell to the task of ensuring that his men were safe as soon as his feet hit the sand.

The breeches buoy was dismantled and the line was cut, perhaps to float ashore later or more likely to be tangled in the sinking rigging, which would settle at the bottom of the ocean and likely never be seen again, all at the whim of the ocean and its unpredictable moods.

Sarah stood watching it all unfold, excited and amazed at the accomplishment of these brave men. Tears rolled down her face as she pictured the wives and children of these men finding out that their loved ones were safe. It might be all in a day's work to Erv and his crew, but to Sarah – who had personally been the recipient of their superhuman efforts – it was nothing short of a miracle.

She supplied everyone with hot coffee and biscuits and ham, and all the survivors were seen to. The men were moved to the main cabin. The ship's captain insisted on making his way back out to the beach as soon as things settled a bit in order to survey the damage to his ship. The man stood there staring, as the remnants of what had been his livelihood slowly sunk into the crashing waves. Through the storm he could hardly make out the mast as it listed and waved about. Before long, the ship had totally broken apart and pieces were being either washed ashore or pulled out to sea. Erv stood beside the captain, lending moral support but unable to do or say anything more than what had already been done.

They made their way back up to the house and reported the fate of the ship to the men, who were saddened, but at the same time deeply grateful to be alive. He informed his men that in the following few days they would salvage what they could; although in their hearts they knew that most of their precious cargo would never be seen again. But, as all good sailors knew, ships and cargo could be replaced, but lives could not. The rest of the day was spent administering first aid to the survivors, drying everyone off and getting them warm and fed.

Now Sarah realized what all the extra beds up in the sleeping quarters were for; but still some of the surfmen found themselves spending the next few nights on the floor, yielding their comfort to that of the rescued men, some injured, who had experienced the trauma. Sarah offered to give up her bed near the kitchen to the men, but no one would hear of it.

As soon as the storm passed, the locals came in force to 'help' with the salvage operation, much of the booty finding its way back to their own homes or boats. The ship's captain shook his head sadly, but realized all too well that he owed his survival and that of his men to the people of the island, and so he looked the other way.

Chapter 15

Within a week, the survivors had all been shipped out and things returned to normal at the Station. Soon the local people, having scavenged all there was to find on the beach, came by to meet any survivors still at the Station. It was then that they discovered a young single woman in the midst of the surfmen. Tongues began to wag immediately. Erv invited all the wives to come and visit with their young survivor. The first to come visit Sarah was a woman named Tilly Downs, their closest neighbor.

The two women took to one another right away. After hugging Sarah and sitting with her, listening as she poured out her heart about her past life, the terrible tragedy and her uncertain future, Tilly came to a decision. Sizing up the situation at the station, she took Sarah's hand in hers. "What has happened to you is an adversity of the worst kind, losing everyone you love and enduring that awful shipwreck! No doubt your entire life is up in the air right now, dear, but you will find that God will show you the way to go if you pray to Him. However right now, for the sake of your reputation – and that of the men – we need to find you some other living arrangements. You do realize that, do you not?"

Sarah nodded reluctantly. "Yes, they have told me the same thing. The problem is that I have nowhere to go, Mrs. Downs. I have no family, no one who is expecting me – no one who wants me, as far as I know..." She hung her head.

Tilly reached up and stroked the girl's cheek with the back of her hand. "You poor little lost sheep! Of course you are wanted – you shall come home with me!"

Sarah's head snapped up; she could not believe the kindness of this total stranger. "But... will that not be an imposition on you and your family?"

Tilly laughed, a gentle tinkling sound that Sarah would come to love. "'Tis just me alone at home, Sarah. I have been a widow these twenty years now and I live by myself. I would be most happy to have the company of another woman." Her sweet smile assured Sarah of the truth behind the words.

Sarah's eyes opened wide. "A widow for twenty years? How have you lived, a woman alone all this time? How have you managed to make a life out here in this rough, desolate place?"

A wry smile settled on Tilly's face. "You never know what you can do until you have to do it, dear girl. I am by nature a stubborn woman and nobody has ever been able to convince me that I cannot take care of myself – at least so far! Though a few have tried, I must admit!" She glanced over at Erv.

Sarah looked over her shoulder as Erv stood laughing and stoking the fire in the kitchen cook stove. "But... I hate to leave Erv and Josiah – that is, the surfmen; they have been so good to me. They took me in as if I were family to them!" Sarah's heartstrings tugged at the thought of moving away from their kindness. She had wrapped herself up in their protection as a barrier against all outside forces, natural and otherwise.

"The surfmen help everyone who needs help, Sarah, and while they have no doubt become protective of you and attached to you, you simply cannot live here," Tilly said gently. "Even way out here in the wilds of the Outer Banks we have a right way and a wrong way to do some things. These stations are built for men only to live here, as I am sure you have discovered. It is hardly a place for *married women*, much less a woman in your situation."

Sarah tilted her head. "I had not thought of it like that. They have partitioned off a place in the kitchen for me to sleep," she said, pointing to a makeshift room divider in the corner, "and they sleep upstairs, so nothing is improper about that... But no doubt you are right." She sighed heavily. "I shall talk to Erv and Josiah and I will let you know right away."

"You go do that right now, child. I will not be leaving here without you this day if you agree to come. And besides that, whenever I visit I bring a few supplies and homemade items to the surfmen and I need to put those away. Just let me know when you are ready and I will help you pack up whatever meager possessions you have."

Sarah corralled Erv right away and he, learning the reason for the conversation, went out and brought Josiah in to be a part of it. They all sat by the fire.

"So, you will be leaving us, then?" Josiah asked sadly. "We have got used to having you around, Miss Sarah." He glanced at Erv. "Our mealtimes have been much improved, along with the company."

"Cannot argue with that," Erv said good-naturedly. "But Tilly is right, I'm sorry to say. You need to get yourself out of here before people begin to talk. Folks here do love to gossip and in the winter 'tis their main source of entertainment. We hate to lose your company, 'tis true, but 'twill be for the best. Our District Supervisor will be coming here soon and he would not expect us to have a woman around, especially an unmarried one as young as you are." He looked at her with sadness and obvious affection. "You are an easy one to love, Lass, and we will miss you!"

Sarah swallowed and began to sniffle.

"But you shall be only a short ride away," Josiah said happily. "We do see Tilly often and no doubt we will be seeing much of you if you decide to stay around these parts!"

Sarah nodded, sniffed and rubbed her hands together nervously. "I do need to ask your advice about one thing before I leave," she said. "What should I do about the money, the gold? Should I give it to Tilly?" She looked back and forth between the men.

Erv laughed. "Tilly's man left her set up well; she is lacking in nothing. So, if you decided to help her out around the place with work, you will be doing more than earning your keep. No, my advice is this: Hide that money in a safe place, stay here through the winter because the days are short and harsh and travel is difficult, and by spring you will have decided what to do with your life and your little fortune."

Sarah looked at both of them and smiled – how she would miss them! "I would like to give you – that is, the station – some of the money if you do not mind, in return for my keep while I have been here. Will you take some, please?"

"No," Erv said flatly. "You have earned every bite that went into your mouth and more besides! We have all that we need here and all of us make a wage that we have no place to spend, even if we wanted to. The government provides for us and we could not in good conscience take anything that belonged to you; you have worked hard yourself in your time here. You keep that money, Miss Sarah. It shall be gone soon enough, believe me." He wagged a finger in her direction.

She considered for a moment and then nodded. "Well, if you feel that is the right thing to do, then that is what I shall do. You have both been wise and helpful to me in every way, so I value your advice dearly. I will put my few belongings in the chest if you will carry it out to the wagon for me."

"Happily," Josiah said. "Well, not happily," he added, looking down, "but willingly."

Erv's pointer finger went up again for emphasis. "Mind what I told you about the money, Sarah dear, and find a safe spot to hide it when you get to Tilly's place. Folks around here are honest for the most part, but if word gets out that you have gold – well, there are a few roundabouts who might not be above wanting to relieve you of some of it."

Chapter 16

Sarah looked around at Tilly's house; even by Ohio standards it would be considered a nice home. The furniture, though not new, was obviously of good quality; the heavy drapes and sturdy rugs underfoot gave the home a warm feeling of coziness.

"My, my, your home is lovely, Tilly," Sarah said. "I was not expecting something this nice – I mean way out here!"

Tilly smiled and nodded. "Yes, it is probably one of the nicer houses on the whole island. My husband built it before we married and it has held up well because it was sturdily built. He was much older than me and not an easy man to live with," she said, making a strange face. "But I have to admit that when he died, he left me well provided for. Folks 'round here were betting that I would be running back to my mother in Maryland, but I have proved them wrong! I have been well satisfied and wanted for nothing in the twenty years that Mr. Downs has been gone. Even though I live alone, I have managed well enough."

"That was good of him..."

Tilly snickered. "Well, he no doubt believed that *he* would be the one enjoying all his wealth, and I know that the thought of leaving everything to me was not one that he ever envisioned. But as they say, 'you cannot take it with you,' can you?" She looked around and smiled. "As you can see, I have plenty of room for you and perhaps a few other people. But do not be spreading that part around because there are few people indeed that I would want to share a home with!" Tilly laughed and rolled her eyes.

"How did he die, your husband?" Sarah asked. "If you do not mind me asking about it, that is..."

Tilly got a distant look on her face. "I shall tell you about it sometime when we are trapped inside by the weather and beginning to go stir crazy… For now, please put your things in the room upstairs at the end of the hall. I believe that you will like that room; it has a nice prospect out to the south."

Sarah went over and touched Tilly's arm. "Thank you again, Tilly… I do not think I could have made a decision about where to go or what to do at the present time, I am that confused and uncertain. So I am grateful that you cared enough to do it for me."

The older woman smiled. "I do have a tendency to take over and be a bit bossy, but that is what living alone for so long does to a woman; I think for myself. But if you should find that I am getting a bit too bossy – and that will probably happen – then just ask me to keep my own counsel!"

Sarah gave her a big hug; both of them enjoyed the rare feeling of being held for a moment. As she watched Sarah mount the stairs, Tilly realized that she had already smiled more today than she had in many months. And while she had settled her mind on living alone, this young woman's company was proving to be quite a tonic for her own spirits.

Chapter 17

Sarah's room did indeed have a pleasant view out the windows on two sides. She could see the waves on the Atlantic above the dunes to the left, as well as the reedy marshes winding around toward the Sound toward the right. In the distance she could just make out the observation platform on Big Kinnakeet Station, a comforting sight.

As she watched the afternoon sun slowly descending toward the horizon, she realized the truth of what Erv and Josiah had told her; she was indeed starting her life again fresh, with no links to the past or expectations for the future. She found the possibilities quite overwhelming.

Goosebumps ran up both her arms and she rubbed her hands over them to try to warm up. It wasn't cold in the room, it was the thought of facing life without her mother, without the Saltmans, to show her the way. She had spent her life following instructions, no questions asked, having to make no major changes on her own. Now it was only her. She would make the decisions and she would face the consequences; her childhood was over. After getting her few belongings settled, she went back downstairs to help Tilly, who was working on supper.

"Hope you like fish," Tilly called out.

Sarah laughed. "Well, I do – I did – even before I came here. But I certainly had no idea that it could be prepared in so many different ways! Erv showed me all the recipes they have over at the station, not just for fish but also for crabs and all the other things you find around here."

Tilly nodded. "And do not forget the oysters! They are my particular favorite and besides roasting them, which everyone does,

I have about a dozen other ways to fix them that will make those slimy little things melt in your mouth!"

"I am eager to learn whatever you are pleased to teach me. Beggars can't be choosers, Tilly," Sarah responded.

Tilly put down her large spoon and walked over to face the girl. Taking her by both arms, she said, "Now you look here, young lady; you get that out of your head right now, do you understand me? You are a smart young woman who could probably accomplish anything you set your mind to. I have only known you a short while and I have already figured out that much! And you are no beggar – you are my guest until you decide what you want to do with yourself. Do you understand?"

Tears formed in Sarah's eyes, but she lifted her chin and refused to let them fall. "Do you truly think that I could accomplish something, Tilly? I am so afraid, so unsure of myself. And you are far too kind to me. I shall never be able to fully repay you for all you are doing for me... but I will try to be a good guest and be helpful in any way that I can."

Tilly smiled and shrugged. "Why not give it at least six months? You are under no pressure here and the weather will have turned back pleasant by then. Edward and I were married such a short time and I had no children, but I have always wanted a daughter. So you are giving me an experience that I have desired for a long time. Not that I plan to mother you, now. You are a little too old for that! But I will enjoy your company."

"I will do my best not to be a lot of bother, but..."

Tilly put her hands on her hips. "Erv and I are old friends. He dropped by to see me yesterday and told me of your situation. He told me what kind of girl you are and how lost you are feeling. I believe he knew that this arrangement would be a good thing for both of us." She smiled warmly. "And I think so, as well!"

During a quiet afternoon the following day Sarah asked Tilly if she had any needles and thread. Her own dress had taken a real beating in the ocean and the few other pieces she had chosen from what Erv called 'the rag pile' were also in need of mending and a little adjustment to fit her.

Tilly provided her with a lovely sewing basket full of all kinds of threads, needles, ribbons and odds and ends. "Can you sew well?" she asked as she handed Sarah the basket.

"Yes... I suppose. My mother taught me since I was small and it is second nature to me. If fact, it was my job to make all the girls' clothing in the house and also to mend the men's things. If I got my hands on some nice material, I could think of a dozen ways to make a beautiful dress out of it. The Saltmans' store carried a goodly supply of fabric. In fact, I have made dresses for other ladies as well – and been paid for it, too!" She smiled proudly. "Mrs. Saltman used to say that my sewing was the finest gift that God had given me."

"Well now, that is surely a blessing from on high! My husband bought that sewing basket shortly after we were married; I think that he was under the mistaken impression that I would grow into the kind of wife who could sew beautifully..." She snickered. "But I have always been more of an outside person, and I am afraid that sewing is a skill that I never cultivated. I tried, but..." she shrugged. "He learned fairly quickly that I was in no danger of becoming a fine seamstress!"

"Then I shall be happy to do any sewing you might need! Do you have any mending that needs doing?"

"Only a pile this high!" Tilly said, holding her hand down by her knees.

Sarah smiled, thinking of the kindness shown to her by these strangers in so many ways. She grabbed the sewing basket and said, "Then I shall work hard and pray that you can put up with me until next year's pleasant weather comes. In the meantime, you *must* give me something to do – I simply abhor sitting around doing nothing and feeling useless. Just show me where that pile of clothing is!"

Tilly gave her a crooked grin. "Be careful what you ask for, dear girl, you might just get it!"

Sarah studied this warm, loving woman. Tilly was probably in her late forties or early fifties, she guessed. The few gray streaks that ran through her dark hair seemed to somehow highlight her bright blue eyes. She dressed well and wore her hair up in a feminine style; a simple diet along with lots of work had kept her trim and fit. Even now, she was an attractive woman, although she certainly didn't seem to know it.

Living with her would be a good thing, giving Sarah the time to grow up and learn so much that she needed to know...that a grown woman needed to know.

Chapter 18

Sarah began to settle in, learning the ways of an Outer Banks homestead and recording it all in her journal. If not for the terrible recurring dreams, she could declare herself quite content. Many nights she would awaken screaming – Tilly would be shaking her and calling her name until she came around. Then she would cling to the older woman, crying her heart out until she settled down and could consider sleep.

It was the *voices* in the dreams that were the worst part... the screams and shouts of the dying as that sound melded with the howling wind; the rolling, crushing waves, the sounds of the boards cracking as the ship broke apart, splintering and sinking into the depths... It all merged into a cacophony of painful noise that dug painful gouges into her heart as she watched the faceless bodies sink down into the cold water, again and again. Recalling the deep fear of facing almost certain death – it was all too much for her conscious mind to deal with, so her dreams tried to sort it all out as she slept.

The day following those dreams she would be emotionally and physically exhausted, unable to eat or function normally, reliving some of the same things she had felt the day after the surfmen had dragged her ashore. If only she could free herself from the tyranny of the dreams, perhaps she could begin to see some kind of future for herself.

Tilly had encouraged her to talk about it – to get the feelings out. Sarah was not ready yet; she felt something akin to anger, but it was not directed at anyone; she felt rage, fear and the deepest loss of all, grief. Keeping that tangled wad of emotions inside and working hard not to face it seemed easier somehow than talking about it, at least for now.

As fall began to give way to winter, Sarah and Tilly worked hard to prepare for the dark, long days ahead. They worked on laying compost on the garden; they tightened down any loose boards or roof shingles they could find. They set everything in the yard and outbuildings to rights as best they could to winterize and protect it.

One day Sarah came in from a brief trip to the outhouse. "By golly, it is cold out there! I would think that I was still in Ohio if not for all the sand! How can it be this cold here in the Carolinas?" she asked, hurrying over to the fire to warm herself.

Tilly laughed. "Prepare yourself, girl, this is nothing to what is coming. This is *North* Carolina, remember, and we get snow and icy cold here even though we are on the beach. 'Tis the wind that hurts the worst," she added, putting on the kettle for a cup of tea. "Seems like it cuts right through whatever coat or hat you are wearing and then tries to blow your clothes right off your body! When we get a nor'easter, you will think that this island is going to disappear under the water, and sometimes part of it does. But so far, we just keep hanging on and life continues... This past summer we suffered the edge of a big hurricane, and then came that big blow that wrecked your ship and blew you ashore. But it has not been a bad year, all in all."

"Yes, Erv and Josiah told me about some of the storms they have seen hereabouts." She shuddered. "It is hard to imagine how dangerous the sea can be until you have been held in its grasp...it is a nightmarish monster that seems to come from nowhere." Sarah sat down at the table, longing for the warmth of the tea as soon as possible. "So, would this be a good time for you to tell me about your husband Edward?" she asked casually.

Tilly stood still and thought. "I have baking to do now, and afterwards we will be going out to gather more firewood, so no, this is not a good time. Later, perhaps..." She turned dismissively and set to work.

When the water boiled, Sarah set about making the tea. She offered a cup to Tilly, who thanked her and kept working quietly, her mind obviously somewhere else. "I shall take my cup upstairs and work on the sewing for a while, Tilly. The light out the south window is very good this time of day..." the younger woman said.

"Hmmm.... oh yes, whatever you like, dear..." Tilly responded without turning around.

Sarah was beginning to see that whenever she mentioned Tilly's dead husband Edward, Tilly stiffened a bit and grew quiet, reflective. Perhaps the memories were not pleasant ones; it was unfeeling of her to bring them up. She decided to stop asking about him so often – Tilly would tell her if and when she was ready.

Chapter 19

Sarah sat near her bedroom window, enjoying the light. The sun was nearer the southern horizon in the winter and often its glare would almost blind you if you stared directly into it. But the warmth of even distant light was welcome during the short days that they were now experiencing.

Her mending project all done, Sarah decided to take apart some of the badly damaged clothing that she and Tilly had, in order to make newer things to wear. When Erv had heard about her sewing talents, he sent a large pile of salvaged clothing over to her, and told her to make whatever she pleased from it. Today she would cut out a shirt to make for one of the men. The blue wool uniforms the men wore looked quite professional, but they still could use soft shirts underneath as well as long, warm night shirts. She smiled at the thought of presenting the men with gifts.

Josiah had brought the bundle of clothing over one day and lingered around for as long as his conscience would allow him to stay. He had missed Sarah, he told her plainly. As had Erv and Phil. The new surfmen who had been assigned to the station were good enough fellows, he reported, and one of them was a much better cook than Erv, so in some respects life at the station had improved.

But Josiah declared that one of the new men was a real chatterbox, and 'when you are stuck altogether in one house, that can begin to wear on a man', he added. So he had found as much to do outside as possible and used his spare time to continue to work on his drawing, sitting on the dunes.

On one of his visits he brought some of his pictures, ocean scenes for Tilly and Sarah to look at. And even though the paper was rough and the pencil or charcoal was smudged in places, Sarah commented that he had caught the personality of the ocean in all its moods: calmingly peaceful, happily active and bitterly angry. She asked to keep one of the peaceful scenes and hung it on her bedroom wall to remind her that, most of the time, the ocean was a lovely and welcoming neighbor, providing food and work for the sturdy people who were brave enough to live here.

Sarah could hardly bring herself to look at one particular drawing Josiah had showed them; that one perfectly portrayed the sea in all its dark fury, a boat floundering on sandbars in the distance and bodies – some dead, some stirring to life – on the shore in the driving rain as the surfmen worked. It was not just the sadness of the scene, what struck her was that Josiah had perfectly captured the raging anger of the water, the unending hunger of the depths for more bodies, and the helplessness of the mere humans unfortunate enough to be caught in its grasp. That very same night the dreams returned.

One November day Tilly rushed upstairs and interrupted Sarah's sewing. "We must get ready, I believe a storm is coming in," she said.

"What shall I do?"

Tilly began to count things off on her fingers. "We will go outside and make sure that the animals are put up securely first. Then we will move anything that might blow away, put it inside the house or the barns and secure everything else. Then we will gather enough food and water for several days. We also must get the ladder and close the outer shutters on all of the windows and doors. I will cook up what I can before the storm gets here. The house will be dark, but we have the lamps."

Sarah was frightened. "How soon will it be here?"

Tilly shook her head. "Only God knows the answer to that, or to how bad it will be when it does come, and He is not giving us the details. But He *has* given us the good sense to know that the time has come to get prepared, so come on now!" She turned and ran down the stairs like a woman half her age.

Sarah followed Tilly and helped however she could. The wind picked up and the dark skies grew darker as they worked. In the distance she could see the darkness coming closer as the rain poured down out in the ocean. A sudden gust almost blew her over and Tilly indicated that it was now time for them to go inside and stay put.

Chapter 20

Tilly tried to put a face of fun on it once they were inside, and they began cooking up some of their favorite foods to hold them over through the blow. "It's good to stay as busy as possible when stuck inside," she said. "It helps to keep our minds off the things that we cannot control." Sarah wondered how this woman living alone could have faced these storms with such a fearless attitude.

Soon the cooking was done and the rain began to come down in earnest. Sarah worried about the chickens and the pigs and the cows, but Tilly assured her that the barn her husband had built was sturdy enough to withstand any winds that had come along so far, and no doubt it would weather this storm equally well. Still, the plaintive sounds of the cows bellowing could be heard above the wind. The three of them had snorted and swished their tails and generally been uncooperative while they were being put up, but now their fear was evident and the sound of the cows set the pigs to squealing as well.

Sarah picked up her sewing and moved nearer to the lamp. Her hands shook as she tried to work and she repeatedly stuck herself with the needle. Finally, she laid it down and looked at Tilly, whose eyes were cast toward the ceiling and the sounds coming from upstairs.

"Shall I go upstairs and make sure that everything is alright, Tilly?"

"No! Stay right where you are, girl!" Tilly answered sharply, then turning toward the frightened girl she added softly, "This is the safest place in the house and the storm will be over before you know it. We have only to wait it out."

As time crawled by, the shutters rattled and shook, the sounds of things unknown being blown against the house were heard repeatedly, and the howl of the wind was unrelenting. The women moved about as little as possible, only to eat or drink or tuck a different blanket against the bottom of the doors when one became saturated.

When night fell, they attempted to sleep in the living room on mattresses they had brought down from upstairs. As the clock chimed ten, Sarah thought that she heard things begin to quiet down outside and she breathed a sigh of relief. "It is over, then?" she asked Tilly.

Tilly shook her head slowly. "No, Dear. We are simply in the lull, what they call the eye of the hurricane. They say the storms are like a big circle that is clear in the middle," she said, drawing it out in the air with her finger as she explained. "One side passes over you, then the lull, and then the backside comes 'round."

"Is the backside easier?" Sarah asked hopefully.

Tilly exhaled loudly. "No, Sarah, it is often worse. But we have made it this far, and we will survive the rest of the night, I assure you."

Sarah cried, valiantly trying to keep her tears silent; but a few sobs escaped despite her best efforts. Tilly moved over and took her hand gently. "There, there, dear, it isn't so bad – this will be over before we know it!" she said.

Sarah's sobs became louder. "How – how can you stand this? How can you live in this terrible place, Tilly?" she demanded.

This seemed like the perfect time to get the girl's attention elsewhere, so Tilly sat back and got comfortable. "Would you like to know how I came to be here in the first place?" she asked.

Sarah glanced up and her whimpers began to settle down. "Yes, but... do you feel like talking about it now? I do not want to pry..."

Chapter 21

Tilly sighed deeply. Like Sarah, she preferred to keep this memory inside and not think about it, but she knew that her story would get the terrified young girl's mind off the storm. So she took a deep breath and began.

"I was younger than you when my father arranged my marriage to Edward. He was in his forties, near fifty I expect. Now, don't look like that – it was a common thing for fathers to arrange that their daughters marry older men, men who could provide for them. My father saw it as a way to guarantee my future, I suppose. He was involved in shipping and met Edward at the docks. The two of them took to one another right away and before I knew it, I was betrothed to him, never even having met him."

Sarah made a face.

"When Father brought him home to Mother and me, I was quite impressed at first, as was my mother. He was very gentlemanly, well-mannered and despite his age, a fine looking man. Several of my friends had been given in marriage to men who were not nearly as impressive as Edward was, so I felt that all-in-all, my Father had done me a good thing. And like any young girl, the whole idea of being swept away to a new home, all my own, seemed quite romantic."

"Edward told us of the shipping business he had owned and sold in Virginia, the fine home that he had built for himself down here on the Outer Banks… it all seemed like I was moving into a fairy-tale life with a wealthy husband."

"Did you love him?" Sarah asked timidly.

Tilly paused. "I think that I was in love with the idea of love. I hardly knew the man at all, and within a few weeks of meeting him I was married to him. I expected that love would come later; that's what my mother had told me…"

She looked down. "And, like many other young girls, the reality of it did not come near to the romantic vision I had in my head. But I had my fancy wedding, and we set off for what I just knew would be a big adventure. When we boarded the boat in Baltimore, I was surprised to find that it was more of a cargo ship than a fancy passenger liner – which is what I had expected in my dreams, but we waved goodbye to my parents and the ship set sail. We were shown to our cabin, and I was surprised to find that it was little more than a closet with a single bed. But I decided to try to put a positive face on it and knew that the journey was not a long one."

Sarah was entranced by Tilly's story, and the sounds of the storm receded far into the background as she hung on her every word.

Tilly paused for a long moment, took another deep breath and began again. "That first night was… well, let me just say that it was not what I imagined that it would be… it was horrible, in fact. Edward had me undress and then for no reason he began to beat me – oh, not in the face where anyone could see, but in other places that were well concealed."

Sarah gasped. She had never been around such violence.

She lifted her chin and her mouth twitched. "He told me that I was to learn my place at the beginning and not to ever question anything he told me to do – just to do it. Or else. I was in tears, and then he forbade me to ever cry in his presence again, driving home the point by twisting my arm up behind my back and threatening to break it. 'People fall on ships all the time,' he told me. 'No one will think anything of it if your arm gets broken.' So that was the last time I cried, at least when he was anywhere around."

Sarah felt tears falling down her own cheeks.

"There I was, naked and in tears and in pain, and he forced himself on me. I was made to sleep on the floor when he was done with me, and for the rest of the trip. I was locked in the cabin and humiliated in every possible way on that boat trip to the Outer Banks, so by the time we got here I did not have any fight left in me. That was the way our marriage started, and that was the way it went for the eighteen months that I had to endure his presence."

Sarah grabbed Tilly's hands. "Oh, Tilly, I cannot imagine how awful you must have felt; so scared, so alone…"

Tilly laughed, a sad little sound. "Actually I learned very quickly not to feel anything. I shut down that part of myself, burying it deep and I became little more than a body, doing what I was told and never, ever allowing myself to feel. He had run me down so far that I felt worthless – that's what he told me constantly."

"But somewhere deep down all of those feelings began to turn to rage. I knew that if I ever let that anger out, I would kill him. And I seriously considered doing that, although I knew that I could never really murder anyone. But words cannot describe how… how tortured and imprisoned he had me here, in every possible way."

"Did you never try to escape, to go home?"

"Escape? The man knew where I was at all times. He wrote letters on my behalf to my parents, telling them that we were happy and getting along well down here. My parents would write back, asking if they could come visit or if I could please write them a few words myself, but Edward always made up some excuse or another. They had their suspicions, but they were so far away… Edward was a powerful man, and no one would dare to cross him in any way. So I was stuck here."

"He worked me like a slave during the day and humiliated me at night. I am so very grateful that I did not conceive a child – I would not have brought a child into that man's presence. I would have had to kill Edward first, before making him a father." She shook her head. "But as things turned out, I was spared that duty."

"What happened?"

Tilly almost smiled. "We had a terrible wind come up; Edward went out to survey the damage. Suddenly a powerful gust came and a tree was blown over, right on top of him. I heard him hollering and ran outside. He was severely injured; I knew that much. He couldn't move his legs. He was screaming at me to move the tree, get help, do something... He cursed me and threw a rock he could reach at me, promising to kill me if I didn't get moving. My head was bleeding from where the rock had hit me. I went toward the barn automatically to saddle the horse, because I knew that I could never move that tree alone and that he needed a doctor."

"When I walked into the barn, the horse, who was just as abused as I was, nuzzled me. He was my only friend, really; Edward did not allow me to have visitors unless he had invited them. So I sat down on a bale of hay and began to talk to the horse, totally shutting out his screams for help. I told the horse all about the abuse I had suffered from that man, and he seemed to be listening and almost – understanding. Edward treated that animal abominably. Once I started talking, I must have gone on for over an hour, talking, crying, no doubt I was a real mess." She shook her head. "But after I had finished, I felt so much better – almost giddy. I hung my arms around the horse's head and we comforted one another."

"Then it was as if – somehow – I came alive again. I began to truly *feel* something for the first time since coming here. I thought of Edward, laying out there under that tree and I began to laugh. I must have laughed for five minutes, until I couldn't get my breath anymore."

She looked up. "I hope that you do not think badly of me for what I did, but... when I went outside to check on him, he was still fuming, and I noticed blood coming from his nose and mouth. When I bent down to check on him, he mustered up the last of his strength to curse and then slapped me."

Sarah gasped, covering her mouth with her hand. "What – what did you do?"

Tilly sat back. "I went inside and made a cup of tea. I knew where he kept his brandy and I even put some of that in it. Then… I sat down and drank the tea. I tidied up the kitchen, sat down with my favorite book, and … waited. Soon I noticed that I heard no more noises. After a few hours, I went out and checked on him again. By that time, he was unconscious. I looked at him; the hate on his face was frozen there and I shall never forget that look. I turned, came back inside and read some more of my book. A few hours later I saddled the horse and went to the nearest neighbor's house, pleading for help."

"When we got back, Edward was dead. I neglected to tell them exactly when the tree had fallen. Everyone was solicitous and kind, offering to help in any way they could, so I let them take his body inside and help me dress it for a wake and then burial."

"Did anyone know how he had treated you, what kind of person he really was?"

Tilly shook her head. "He was well thought of all around, respected and looked to as a leader in the community. He acted ever the gentleman when others were around. I decided to simply let that be, and played the part of the grieving widow. Everything that was his now belonged to me. I knew where he kept his gold because he would take it out in front of me and count it. The thought never occurred to him that I would ever challenge him in any way."

"How could he be so cruel to you?" Sarah asked, shaking her head.

Tilly thought about the question. "I do not believe that Edward saw women as real people, merely as property. He took me out down the beach one time and pointed to the dunes and said, 'I had a negro slave who served me before you came. She got herself pregnant several times, and every time I got rid of the bastard right after it was born. The last time she died in childbirth. I buried her there, and I will bury you here if you ever disobey me.' He said it so simply, with no emotion – I knew that he meant it."

"He killed – his own – children?"

Tilly nodded. "They were half negro, and he would never have allowed his bloodline to be tainted like that. I am just so very grateful that I never had his child!"

Sarah sat back and was quiet for a long time. Tilly looked at her. "If you think badly of me for letting him die, I understand. It was a very unkind, selfish thing to do. But I have come to the conclusion that I could have done nothing else. If he were crippled, I could not have borne the abuse he would have heaped on me. If he had survived, I would have died myself..."

Sarah reached for Tilly and took her in her arms. "No one on this earth or in heaven could have blamed you, Tilly. You did not kill the man, after all. And you can be sure that I will never, ever repeat this story. You are a better person than many of us would have been in those same circumstances. I do not understand how you put up with it for as long as you did."

Tilly drew back and made a strange face. "As women, we have few choices in life, you will learn this. But I did make the choice to never marry again, and I am sure that you understand why."

Sarah nodded. "I promise never to bring the man's name up again," she said.

Tilly laughed. "He is buried out near the sound, but you will not stumble across his grave. His fancy tombstone 'fell over' and has been long since covered with sand. No one will have to encounter that man ever again!"

Chapter 22

While they were talking, the wind had picked up again and the backside of the storm had been bearing down on them. Tilly was right, it seemed even more fierce – more loud, the rain heavier – than even the first part of the storm. Sarah prayed quietly for them as well as for Erv, Josiah and all the other brave people who lived out in this wild area. It did seem to pass more quickly than the first part, as Tilly had foretold.

During the wee hours of the morning they sensed that the storm had fully passed over. The wind, while still blowing, was now a constant low sound, not the pounding, crazed, howling monster that it had been before. Exhausted, the two women finally fell asleep.

When Sarah awoke the next morning, Tilly was bustling about. "Come outside with me and let us determine the damage done," she said to her young friend. When they opened the front door and unlatched the inside of the two shutters, Sarah could hardly believe what she saw. The neat yard they had so carefully emptied of anything that might blow around was now full of debris: downed branches from trees, odds and ends blown away from someone else's home and now in their yard, along with water at least six inches deep and more in some places.

They followed the porch around the side of the house and looked out toward the Sound. Sarah gasped. The water was deeper out that way than in the front yard and seemed to stretch toward the reedy grasses, which were themselves now half covered. The barn, which had been built on ground a little higher, seemed to be surrounded by water but not flooded as far as they could tell.

"The storm must have moved up the Sound and pushed its water inland," Tilly said, taking stock of the situation. "All in all, thank

God, we have survived with very little damage." She put her hands on her hips and looked around. "Yes, all in all, we did not fare too badly."

"This is good?" Sarah exclaimed. "How is this," she said extending her hand around, "good in any way?"

Tilly turned and looked at her. "We are alive, are we not? We still have a roof over our heads and our livestock is unharmed! No doubt there will be some damage to the house and the barn, but believe me, Girl, it could have been – and has been – much, much worse!"

Sarah hung her head. "Forgive me, Tilly, I do not mean to be ungrateful, it's just that…that…it was so very awful!" She lifted her chin and tried to hold back the tears.

Tilly walked over and gave her a hug. "Now, now. No doubt it is all the bad memories you have from the storm that took your ship, child. You have not gotten over the fear, the terror that you experienced." She stepped back, holding Sarah at arm's length. "It is the price of living here, part of what we experience on the Outer Banks. While we do get used to it, we are always afraid, all of us. Too many have died in these storms for us to not be fearful. And the stupid people who do not fear are the ones who die first. But look," she said, waving her hand toward the sky, "the sun is shining and the sky is clear and blue as if it never happened."

Sarah looked around. Sure enough, the earth was bouncing back quickly and things would be going on and on. She laughed a little and asked. "How is that even possible? The weather was the same way after the storm that brought me here! As if there had been no storm at all!"

Tilly crossed her arms and looked around. "I believe it is God's way of telling us that life goes on, Sarah, and so must we. If we let the fear conquer us and stop us from living, then our lives will have no meaning. Instead, we have to put all this behind us, be grateful for what we have left and move on." She looked down. "The next time we go for supplies we are getting you a decent pair of boots! Real boots, not those silly lady boots, but the ones like the fishermen wear. I have only the one pair and I will be wearing them. Yes, you are definitely going to be needing boots!"

Sarah looked down at her sad little half boots and began to laugh. Wading around in all that water in these would be a chore, but she would do it. Her laughter rolled on and soon both of them were laughing so hard that they collapsed against each other until they had laughed themselves out. They recovered and set to work.

Watching the older woman work with a smile on her face, Sarah was awestruck at her resilience, her determination to be in control of her life. There was a lot that she could learn from Tilly Downing, and she intended to do just that.

Chapter 23

Later that day, Erv and Josiah came riding up on the wagon pulled by the big dray horse from the station. The standing water had gone down some, but still they slogged along until they came to Tilly's house, jumped off onto the porch and tied the horse to the porch posts. "Anybody home?" They shouted.

Sarah came out the front door drying her hands on a towel. "Erv! Josiah! How wonderful to see you, I was so worried about you!" She threw her arms around each of them in turn, hugging them fiercely. "Thank God you are both alright!"

Josiah blushed as she removed her arms from around his neck. He didn't want to let her go; he had been equally worried about her. He gave her a little squeeze and then released her. She looked up at him and smiled.

The young man cleared his throat and used his 'official' voice. "Yes, well, we left the others at the station and headed out to check on everyone." He looked around. "Looks like you did not fare too badly here... Is Tilly alright?"

"Yes, she went to the barn to check on and feed the animals. She is the one with the boots, so she would not let me get out in the deep water." Sarah looked down at her stocking feet. "Although I did help a little. My shoes are inside drying out."

Josiah reached over and grabbed something out of the wagon. "I was thinking about you and realized that you probably had no water boots, so I brought over this pair. They must have belonged to a fisherman with small feet, but they still may be too big for you." He handed them to her.

She took the pair of boots from him and examined them. True, they were old and worn but obviously still had plenty of life left in them. She looked at him and gave him her most beautiful smile. "They are... lovely! Thank you, Josiah!"

He grinned. "Well, *lovely* would not be the word that I would choose, but I thought that perhaps you might need them if you were planning to stay on the Banks for a while..." He let the question hang in the air and raised his eyebrows.

"You could not have given me a nicer gift; they are indeed just what I need to live here for... however long I stay. How kind of you to think of me!" She dropped the boots and threw her arms around him and gave him a much longer hug this time.

"Ahem..." Erv said. "Tis just a pair of boots, Miss Sarah, you needn't be quite so grateful! And 'twas partly my idea as well, you know. No need to get carried away here!" He cleared his throat loudly.

Sarah released Josiah and backed away, blushing. "Of course, forgive my silliness please, I was simply... overcome by your thoughtfulness, both of you – and relieved that you are well. Please do come inside and let us feed you. We have cooked all this food that needs to be eaten."

Erv looked over to see Josiah standing just as Sarah had left him, with the largest grin and stupidest look on his face that the older man had ever seen on him. *Oh, no, here we go...* he thought.

The men recounted to them how the station had come through relatively unscathed, and no ships had been lost in the immediate area as far as they knew. The ladies inquired after their other neighbors, but the men had come straight here and had not checked on anyone else yet. Tilly and Sarah fed the two men until they could hold no more, then put together a package of cooked food for them to take along. Josiah could not seem to take that stupid grin off his face for the life of him and Erv promised to share some of the food with the other surfmen. At last the older man managed to drag Josiah away and they got back on the road.

Chapter 24

As the two surfmen rode along, checking on the locals, they discovered that most had fared well enough through the storm; some property damage but no lives lost or serious injuries. The overwash had come up from the Sound and not from the ocean, which meant that salt water had not washed onto their garden plots and other ground, so things would still grow well in the spring. They returned to the station about dark and settled in for the night.

After dinner, Erv slid into his regular chair beside Josiah, who sat staring into the fire, with that same big grin hardly faded from his face. "Are you on duty tonight, Josiah?" he asked the younger man.

Josiah looked up with a blank stare. "What? Duty? Oh, duty... not tonight, Erv, I have beach patrol tomorrow morning first thing. Guess we shall see then what the storm washed up," he said absentmindedly.

Erv looked him over and shook his head. "You have truly got it bad, boy, don't you?"

"What?" Josiah said, finally turning to face him. "Got what?"

Erv gave him a 'you really have no idea, do you?' look. "The girl, Sarah. You have got tender feelings for our Sarah, as any fool can see!"

"What? No, I like her just fine and all, but...I ain't got nothing bad for nobody!" he answered indignantly, not able to look Erv in the eye.

"I may be old, son, but I am neither blind nor stupid. You are in love with that girl. Go on and admit it to yourself and be done with it!"

Josiah looked shocked. "Love? No, no, I..." He paused. "How does a man *know* if he is in love, Erv?"

Erv shifted around uneasily in his chair, looking for a way around that question. "I would be the wrong man to ask about that particular thing. Perhaps one of the other men – Sam there was married for a few years before his wife died. Ask him. He likes to talk about anything, so he will tell you if he knows."

Josiah stared into the fire. "Let me think on it, for a while anyway. I have nothing to offer a girl, especially one as special as Sarah is. Maybe it is just something that will pass over me and I will be back to normal soon."

Erv grunted.

Sam had overheard his name and came over. "Ask me what?" he said, taking a chair. "What you want to know?" Good natured as he was, Sam considered himself an expert on all things and was always eager to share his wisdom.

Josiah started to get up. Erv said to him, "Sit down, boy." He turned to Sam. "You was married for a time were you not, Sam?"

He nodded. "Yep. Happiest three years of my life. If only my sweet Annabelle had lived, we would have a house full of kids by now... but she was taken from me as she tried to birth the first one. Lost both of them that day, I did." He looked down sadly.

"Well, then," Erv said, "Josiah here wants to know what 'tis like to be in love, so if you were all *that* taken with your wife maybe you could tell him ..."

Sam stretched his skinny neck out, threw back his head and laughed. He looked straight at Josiah. "Nobody can tell you what love is like, boy, you just know it when you feel it!" He thought for a moment. "Do you think about her all the time?"

"Well, quite often..."

Erv smothered a laugh.

Sam nodded. "When you think about her do you think about taking her in your arms and kissing her?"

Josiah blushed and shuffled his feet around, looking guilty. "Not every time, but, well, most of the time, I guess..."

Sam went on. "And do you see yourself living with her and having a bunch of children running around underfoot?"

Josiah sat up straight. "Children! No, I...well...," His rugged, sun weathered face blushed deeply. "I *can* see myself being with her all the time."

"And how does she feel about you?"

Josiah looked stumped and shrugged. "I am not sure."

Erv spoke up. "Well, I am. She is just as crazy about you as you are about her!"

Josiah looked pleased but puzzled and asked, "How can you tell that about a woman? *How can you ever know what any woman is thinking?*"

Erv laughed. "True, I do not know what she is thinking; but like I said before, I am neither blind nor stupid, and I can see clearly the way she looks at you, like you are some kind of hero in a storybook. She gets that same glassy-eyed look on her that you've got right now. And," he said, leaning forward and pointing toward the young man, "she hugged you – twice! A girl would not do that unless she was more than fond of you!"

"She hugged you, too!" Josiah responded quickly, pointing back at him.

"Once! And not like she hugged you! Yes, I definitely think that our Sarah likes you more than you know!" He leaned back in his rocker, satisfied that his point had been well made and fully proven.

"Yep," Sam said. "Sounds like love to me! Let me tell you about what it was like when I first met my Annabelle..." He leaned back in his chair and crossed his arms.

The two other men settled in for what they knew would be a long story with many more details than they would care to hear, for Sam was a fearsome talker. But Josiah couldn't keep his mind on Sam's words; he kept pondering the possibility that Sarah might think of him as he thought of her – what a miracle that would be!

Chapter 25

Sarah tried on her new boots. With a few pairs of socks, they'd be just fine. She took them off, held them close and smiled, smelling the paraffin that Josiah had recently applied to them. Yes, she was definitely glad to be alive, she decided. She sat for a long time, cradling the old boots as if they were a baby.

Tilly could see that the time had come to have a little talk with Sarah. Like Erv, she was neither blind nor stupid and had come to the same conclusion about the two young people. The innocent girl had no idea what was happening to her, and it had fallen to Tilly to talk her through those feelings she must be having. Well, she was no expert, but she had figured out a few things during her life... so she would give it a try.

As they sat in the kitchen sharing a cup of tea, Tilly said, "May I ask you a personal question, dear?"

"Of course," Sarah answered, nodding. "You are my dearest friend! You may ask me anything you like!"

Tilly smiled. "I am so happy that we are friends. And friends help each other, do they not? So may I please ask you – how do you feel about our friend Josiah?"

Sarah looked confused. "How I *feel about him*? I am happy to have his friendship. And certainly grateful to him for dragging me out of the surf and saving my life. He is, in all respects, as fine a man as I have ever known."

"Not what you *think* of him, Sarah, but how you *feel* about him, that is what I asked."

Sarah stared down into her teacup. "I am very fond of him, I suppose. As are you..." she said, looking up at Tilly.

Tilly exhaled heavily; this was slow going. "Yes, I am very fond of both Josiah and Erv and I do consider all of the surfmen to be my friends. But from what I have observed, you seem to have a special fondness for Josiah – and he for you, as well."

Sarah's eyes opened wide. "Do you mean that he – he cares for me? As in a 'sweetheart' kind of way? Do you think so, really?" She got a dreamy look on her face and smiled a faraway kind of smile.

"Well, right now I am trying to determine if *you* think of *him* in that way. Do you? Are you in love with him?"

Sarah fidgeted nervously and her pale cheeks turned bright pink. "I... I do not know exactly. I like him very much, but... I am not certain that I know what it is to be in love..."

Tilly laid her hand on top of the younger woman's. "Do you think of him often? Do you dream of him at night? Do you long to see him, to be with him?"

Sarah looked uncomfortable but nodded. "Yes, I suppose I do, Tilly."

Finally, we're getting somewhere! "Well, that is definitely infatuation, which means that you are *beginning* to fall in love. So now you must be very careful around him. If his intentions toward you are serious, then he will treat you with great respect and never take advantage of your innocence."

"Josiah always treats me with respect!"

Tilly nodded. "And that is as it should be. However, you must get to know him very, very well if you are even to consider marrying him."

"Marrying him! I am too young!" Sarah began, but then realized how many girls in these parts were years younger than her and were already married with children. "I mean, I don't feel that I am ready to be a wife, to have children, to run a household, to live with a man…" She covered her eyes with her hands.

Tilly laughed gently. "No one is ever ready for all of that Sarah. It is simply what happens when two people fall in love: marriage, children, problems… all of it. Then they learn as they go along how to handle the things that life throws at them. At least, that is how it is supposed to work."

Sarah was simply amazed that, with her history, Tilly could have any kind of positive view of marriage. "My mother and Mrs. Saltman never spoke to me about these things, Tilly."

"Do you think perhaps the Saltmans expected you to marry one of their older sons?"

Sarah looked as if the thought had never come up into her head. "But the oldest one was just my same age, and he was always like a brother to me – all of the children were like my younger siblings, really the lot of us grew up together!"

Tilly simply raised her eyebrows.

Sarah was quiet for a moment. "Oh… well, perhaps you are right, Tilly; Mrs. Saltman often said that I was her 'daughter' in a special way, I just never thought that she meant… Well, that question does not really signify now, does it, for all of them are…gone."

"No, but no doubt Mrs. Saltman would have talked with you about it before too long. It seems as though the family loved you, and certainly they would consider you a good match for their boy. However, the point is that we are talking about men and marriage now, and you need to be giving consideration to the idea. From what I have observed, Josiah shows all the signs of being in love with you."

Sarah thought about that. "Signs? What signs do you mean?"

Tilly waved her hand in the air. "He cannot stop smiling and staring at you when he is around; he gets a somewhat... dopey... look on his face, actually."

"And that means that he is in love with me?" Sarah almost laughed.

"Well..." Tilly laughed out loud. "In this particular case, I am going to figure that it does indeed. Erv and I have talked about it, and the two of us agree that the two of you are more than a little fond of one another and need to be giving serious thought to all of this. Here again I do not mean feelings, Sarah, I mean *thought*. A girl cannot simply let herself be swept away by her feelings and lose her good sense because she finds a man attractive."

"Oh. But when Josiah is around, I feel so wonderful that I do not want to do a lot of thinking!" She laughed.

"Yes, and that is why we are having this little chat, dear. Infatuation leads to love, love leads to marriage, and marriage is a serious commitment that, once made, you need to be strong enough to stick to for the rest of your life. You give it some more thought and we shall talk about it again later on, alright?"

"Uh...hmmm...." Sarah said, nodding. Tilly would never let her marry anyone who would be a bad match, she felt sure.

The innocent are often the hardest to reach, Tilly thought. *And for her sake, I hope that I have reached her...*

For the next few weeks, Sarah and Josiah felt a bit awkward when around one another, each not certain about the feelings going through the other's heart. So they kept their conversation on ordinary, everyday things.

Josiah was a man of twenty and five now. He had been a surfman for four years. He could see himself doing this work from now on. The experience of saving a life, of giving assistance at a critical time, well it satisfied him deep down in a way that nothing else ever had. But was he ready to marry? Could he keep his position as a surfman and be married?

Thinking of all the other surfmen he had heard of, he realized that a few of the Keepers at other stations were married and also had children. Their families lived on the property, as did the families of the lighthouse Keepers at the Lighthouses. But this was not a common situation in the Life Saving Service, and Josiah was not the Keeper of his life saving station. So it could be a long time before he found himself in the position to even offer for Sarah. He decided to put the prospect out of his mind for the time being.

But that proved to be somewhat harder than he had thought it would be...

Chapter 26

Spring had finally come to Hatteras Island; the flowers were beginning to bloom, and the rough, cold winter was giving over to warmer days. Soon most of the surfmen would be going home for six months, only to come back and sign up for another season again next November. Josiah had stayed with Erv for the summer during his last two years at the station, with only a brief visit home to visit his family. Erv needed his help more each year and he couldn't see this year being any different.

One day as they were all tidying up the place, getting things ready for closing down the station, the surfman on the observation tower called out that a skiff was headed toward the beach, coming from a larger boat that was anchored offshore, apparently heading north. The ship did not appear to be in any distress, he said.

It was not a common thing for them to receive visitors, but occasionally some would drop by or stop in to deliver the odd supplies. Erv got out his sea glasses; he did not recognize this ship, however, and the small boat headed their way seemed to hold only two passengers and little to no cargo.

The available men went down to the beach and helped pull the skiff onshore. Sure enough, it held only two men. One was obviously the boatman and the other was dressed as some kind of gentleman. The gentleman jumped off with no word of thanks to anyone, turned to the boatman and bellowed, "You wait right here until I get back, you understand?"

"Aye." The boatman looked unimpressed with the fellow's bullying ways.

The 'gentleman' turned to the surfmen, who were standing there with questions on their faces.

"Who's in charge here?" he demanded.

The five of them looked toward Erv, who said simply, "That would be me, Erv Brophy; I am the Keeper here at Little Kinnakeet Station. These are my surfmen, Josiah – "

"I don't give a flyin' flea who these other fellas are, it is you that I need to speak with. And now! Where can we go to talk?" he asked, looking around in a manner that spoke disgust for the desolate scene.

"We can take a walk on the beach, or you can come inside if you prefer."

"Yes, and a cup of something to drink would not be asking too much of this pitiful place, would it?" he asked sarcastically. "You do have something to drink, don't you?"

The surfmen exchanged glances. This man had made the worst first impression of anyone who had set foot here in recent history.

Erv looked the smallish man up and down. "Then come back to the station house with us. You other men, go about your business. This is a Thursday, so you can begin setting up the practice for the breeches buoy rescue drill. All but you, Josiah, you come with me." Erv turned and headed back over the dunes.

"No, you and you alone!" the man bellowed, refusing to take a step. "I will not have my private business bandied about as common knowledge!"

Erv turned back slowly, put his hands on his hips and tilted his head. He exhaled heavily, then spoke slowly but firmly. "Whatever brings you here, Sir – and I assume that it is business because you are a stranger to me – will be handled in the presence of my second in command, Josiah Miller. He will be a witness to our conversation. If that arrangement is not acceptable to you," he added, pointing toward the skiff, "you may re-board your dingy and have your boatman take you right back to that ship that brought you here. It is your choice."

The man blustered around and finally began walking toward Erv, without a verbal agreement or acknowledgement. They walked in silence up to the station house. Once inside, Erv handed the man a cup of lukewarm coffee and told him to sit at the table.

The stranger took a sip, almost spit it out and said, "This is the best you got to offer me? How 'bout something a little stronger – that was one devil of a boat ride I had to take to even get to this godawful place!"

Erv ignored his outburst. "What is your name, Sir, and what would your business here be?"

He glared back at Erv. "My name is Silas Beaufort. I am from Charleston, South Carolina." The man's heavy Southern drawl confirmed that part of his story at least. "I want to know if this is the station that *failed to rescue* the ship *Ladybird* when she was shipwrecked here last fall. Well – is this the one?"

Erv and Josiah shared a look. That was the ship that Sarah had come from.

"Yes, it is," Erv said, "and we are also the ones who rescued the only survivor. The rest perished when the ship floundered and broke apart in one of the worst nor'easters that we saw last year. The *Ladybird* was too far gone to save by the time we got to her."

The man seemed unconcerned about any possible survivors. He dismissively waved his hand and leaned forward. "What about the cargo, man? Did you find any kind of cargo, any possessions?"

Erv's eyebrows scrunched together. "Sir, what business could this possibly be of yours? Was the ship or anything on it your property?"

"Yes, well, no...not exactly." Silas Beaufort shifted around in his seat, then sat up straight and leaned forward. For a small fellow, he tried to present himself as a force to be reckoned with. But these surfmen had faced the wrath of the angry sea, so this pompous little man did not impress them at all. "My business partner, Amos Saltman, was on that ship and he was transporting something that was our common business property."

Erv and Josiah shared another glance. "Such as?" Erv asked.

Flustered, Beaufort's face turned red. "Such as personal items, perhaps a trunk or a satchel containing... well, gold! It was half mine; he had purchased a half-interest in my plantation! What happened to all the cargo? Did you let the scavengers take it away or did you keep it for yourself?" he demanded, leaning forward and pounding the table with his fist.

Erv took his time before answering. "Josiah, go get the records and let us see what we recorded as salvage from the wreck of the *Ladybird*." Josiah shook his head, got up and brought the book over right away.

The stranger leaned forward and jabbed his finger onto the tabletop. "I have corresponded with your supervisor, a Mr. Kimball, and he says that there was definitely salvage from the wreck. I want to see it, because it is my property and I have a right to it!"

Sumner Kimball was indeed the Head of the Life Saving Service, based in Washington, D.C. Erv knew that Kimball was not a man who was easily maneuvered, and over half of the politicians in Washington would attest to that fact. If this man had actually been in touch with Kimball, then this was a somewhat official request that Erv could not easily ignore.

Josiah handed the book to Erv, who opened it to the correct page. He scanned down the entries with his finger and said, "Oh, yes, here it is. October 20, 1886, the *Ladybird*. Lost with all hands and only one female survivor."

"*What about the salvage*, man? Was there any – wait, a female survivor?" Beaufort ran a finger and thumb over his skimpy mustache. "Who was the survivor?" Beaufort asked.

Erv pretended to consult the record. "A Miss Sarah Fletcher, who was traveling with the Saltman family according to this, and the only salvage was a chest of her possessions..."

Beaufort looked as if he might smile. "Sarah Fletcher, you say? A chest of her possessions?" Then he laughed aloud. "Yes, Miss Fletcher was to be my wife, so anything that belongs to her belongs to me!" His eyes looked vicious. "And, of course, I will take her, too!"

Josiah sat up straight. Erv put out a hand and touched him on the shoulder. "Get me a cup of coffee, Josiah, and warm it up." The young man looked for all the world as if he wanted to talk back to his boss, but then thought better of it, got up and moved toward the stove.

"And bring me some hot coffee, Boy, this cupful is disgusting!" Beaufort spat.

Josiah's shoulders stiffened. He stood still, but didn't utter a sound, and just went back to the business of warming the coffee.

Erv tried to size up this Silas Beaufort; he was obviously well-to-do, apparently some kind of faded Southern Gentleman. His clothes seemed a bit worn, so the war must have taken some of the stuffing out of this man and his prominence. He looked to be in his early 50's, gray around the temples, with a permanently-etched hateful look on his face. Erv had been sizing men up as part of his job for decades now, and it didn't take long for him to get the full measure of this man. And he didn't like him one little bit!

Erv looked at his notes and said, "Miss Fletcher is staying with one of the local families, who took her in. She told us that she was on her way to South Carolina with the Saltmans, but after the shipwreck she decided to stay here instead of going on. In fact, I believe that we were informed that she has cancelled all plans she may have had to go to South Carolina."

"She cannot do that! She is legally betrothed to me! Her goods are mine! We are to be married!" He slammed his fist down on the table. Josiah turned and gave him a murderous look, which fortunately the smaller man failed to notice.

"Legally betrothed, you say?" Erv asked innocently.

"Yes. Saltman and I worked it all out before they left Ohio. He was to be my new half-partner in my plantation and he was bringing me the gold – and the girl. My first wife died during the war and the second one didn't last much longer, so I need another one, a young one to bear me some white sons. Got a dozen of the other kind," he said, waving his hand in the air, "but they won't inherit nuthin' of mine!"

Erv swallowed his ire. "I assume that you have documentation to prove these claims?"

"Yes, I brought it all with me." He reached inside his jacket and pulled out a leather folder containing a pile of documents, laying it on the table. "It's all right here!" He poked the pile with his finger.

"Well, I'll just take a look, then," Erv said and began to reach for the paperwork.

Beaufort snatched it back. "You will do no such thing!"

"You expect me then to simply *take your word* for all of these claims of yours, Mr. Beaufort?" Erv asked, raising one eyebrow.

The man fumed. "No. But I will show these documents only to those who are legally entitled to look at them. And that is not you! I told Mr. Kimball that I have everything to prove what I was saying and he agreed."

Erv knew Sumner Kimball well and was sure that he would never go along so easily with a plan like that, much less a man like this one. "Mr. Beaufort, I suggest that you go back to Charleston and return when you have legal proof of your claims that you are willing to share with us. Josiah, forget the coffee., this man is going back to his ship!" Erv stood and began to walk away.

Beaufort jumped up. "You cannot do this!"

Erv stopped, turned around and said firmly, "I believe that I just did, Sir. I am the Keeper of the Little Kinnakeet Life Saving Station and what I say goes around here! Please remove yourself from my station and do not show yourself here again until you have written permission for these outrageous demands of yours from Sumner Kimball himself! Now, go!"

Silas Beaufort looked as if he might explode. He grabbed the documents, stuffed them back into his jacket, took hold of the cup of cold coffee and arrogantly dumped it out on the table. He stormed through the door, down the steps and headed outside, hurling curses at everyone he passed.

Erv watched him out the window. "He will probably figure out any minute now that he's headed away from the beach... Oh, there he goes, he's turning around..." After a deep belly laugh, he turned to Josiah, who stood by the stove looking angrier than Erv had ever seen him.

He walked over to the younger man, put his hand on Josiah's shoulder and said, "Now, don't fret, Josiah. I know men, and that man was all bluster and talk. Just trying to lay his hands on something that he was not entitled to. We won't be seeing him again, I wager."

Josiah's upper lip twitched. "But what if he should come back?"

Erv thought for a moment. "Well, I do seriously doubt that he will. But if it happens, we shall deal with it then. Do not worry, Son, he will never marry her."

The young man looked somewhat mollified. "Should we tell Sarah about this?" Josiah asked.

Erv contemplated the question, nodded his head and answered. "I suppose that we should make her and Tilly aware of it. The women need to be warned, in case the fool comes back and tries to go directly to them. We will go over to visit this afternoon after the drill and talk with them."

Josiah nodded, walked out the door and stomped down to the beach. If he had to push the boat out to sea all by himself, he was making sure that Silas Beaufort got off this island!

Chapter 27

The four of them sat around Tilly's table. Erv had brought along a fine bottle of wine, one of the few fringe benefits of being the Keeper of the Station and the man who inventoried the salvage. Surprised, Tilly had simply smiled and poured each of them a glass.

After a little polite conversation, Erv said, "Ladies, we will get straight to the point." He took a long sip, glanced appreciatively at the wine in his glass and then put it down. "We had a visit this morning from a Silas Beaufort..."

"Beaufort! I know that name! He is the one that Mr. Saltman was doing business with down in South Carolina, I believe!" Sarah said, looking surprised.

"Yes, so he told us," Erv said. "Today he came here to recover anything that belonged to the Saltmans, saying that half of it was legally his. Now all of us *know* that is not true, but that is what he claimed."

Tilly looked confused. Erv took a moment to bring her up to date about finding the chest, giving Sarah the gold, and how he had instructed Sarah to tell no one – not even her – about having it.

She nodded. "That was a wise suggestion."

Sarah frowned. "But I did *want* to tell you, Tilly. I told Erv that I do not need the gold, that he could have it, or that you could have it!"

She put her hand on Sarah's. "Now you listen to me, child: You will be needing that gold to build your future life. I speak from experience. If my husband had not left me so well set-up, there is no telling what would have become of me! You may think now that you do not need it, but you will find that a time will come when you do. A woman alone needs money to keep her from becoming a victim to any number of awful happenings!"

Clearly uncomfortable with the Saltman's money, Sarah said to her, "Can I give it to you to keep for me? I have it in my dresser drawer upstairs!"

Erv drew back and said, "I told you to hide it, Lass!"

Sarah looked down. "I am sorry, Erv. I do not even want to touch it. It stills feels as if it does not belong to me, as if I am stealing it from the Saltmans."

Josiah reached across the table and took Sarah's hand in his. She looked up at him, startled at his bold move.

"I have kept quiet until now, Sarah, but I must speak to you about this matter. Beaufort is an evil, greedy man. He is fifty years old if he is a day, and it's not only the money that he wants. When he learned that you survived the shipwreck, well, he..."

"What?" Sarah asked. She did not like the look on Josiah's face one bit.

He gritted his teeth and answered. "The man also claimed that you are betrothed to him and that whatever you have belongs to him. He refused to provide documentation of a marriage contract, but he did seem certain that you were being brought to South Carolina to be his bride."

"Impossible!" she said shaking her head. "The Saltmans never spoke to me about anything like that! They would surely not marry me off and not even tell me about it! No one could be that cruel!"

They all shared a look. Arranged marriages were as common as any other kind, more so in fact, and marriage contracts were legal documents. Sarah was probably the only one at the table who was not aware of this.

Tilly sat up straight, spoke and broke the silence around the table. "The Saltmans may have seen it as a good thing for you, them providing you some security in your future. Perhaps the two men had discussed the *possibility of marriage* and Mr. Saltman wanted to be sure of the man before he spoke to you about it, doing so at the same time he considered the purchase of the plantation share. No doubt they wanted to make sure that he would be a good husband for you. Certainly they knew he could provide for you... but there may not have been an official contract made." She tried to look hopeful.

Sarah saw the troubled look on Tilly's face; she reflected on Tilly's experience and knew that she would never allow herself to fall into that same trap. Never.

Erv nodded and said, "There was nothing that I saw in the documents in that chest of yours that mentioned a marriage, but we will go back over everything to be sure. You are of legal age now and cannot be forced into a marriage, but if there is a legal marriage contract entered into on your behalf by your legal guardian, it must be honored or we must find some legal way out of it. Do not worry, Sarah, we will get everything all straightened out and you will not have to marry this man, I promise you."

Tilly gave Erv a questioning look. Documented marriage contracts, as she well knew, were as binding as any legal agreement. Getting Sarah released from one would not be easy.

"Hopefully that will be the last we see of the man," Josiah said. "I certainly hope that I never see him again, or I cannot be responsible for my actions!"

The three of them turned toward Josiah. "What does *that* mean exactly?" Tilly asked.

He shook his head. "It was all I could do not to pummel him into a bloody little pile today!"

"Now, you don't mean that, Son," Erv said. "You haven't a violent bone in your body!"

Josiah got a firm set to his jaw. "I would do whatever is necessary to protect Sarah from that scoundrel!"

Tilly cleared her throat. "Well, he is probably gone for good, so don't you even be thinking like that, Josiah Miller!"

Josiah hung his head but said nothing. They finished their glasses of wine in the midst of a sadly oppressive silence. Sarah brought down the documents from the chest and together they looked through them, searching for a marriage contract. They found nothing like that. The men said their goodbyes, got up, and returned to the Station.

Sarah watched them ride off. Her heart was full to overflowing with feelings that she was not familiar with: fear of this stranger, anxiety about Josiah's anger, and contempt for the gold that she had unwillingly inherited. Yet at the back of it all, she felt warm and protected by the one woman and two men who had promised to keep her safe, her new family.

Chapter 28

Silas Beaufort got off the ship when it anchored off Nag's Head. He asked around enough to determine that the young female survivor was currently staying, not with a 'family' as he had been told, but with a widowed woman of middle age. People here were eager to share any kind of gossip they'd heard, and Tilly was well known in the area.

He found himself a place to stay up on the northern part of the Outer Banks, in Kill Devil Hills. There he would be near a telegraph as he tried to get his legal issues situated. After thinking it over, he decided to take one more run at it. He had made some small connection with Sumner Kimball and felt that he was armed and ready to go to battle with the two women; how hard could that be after all?

Two days later he boarded a small boat back down to Oregon Inlet, took the ferry and, and rented an old horse to make the rest of the trip. This would be easy enough, he felt sure. Naturally, his superior intellect and abilities would overwhelm the girls and they would be soft clay in his hands. They were only women, after all, one old and the other little better than a child; it would not be like facing those tough surfmen. If everything went according to plan, he would be leaving with whatever gold had been recovered as well as a young new wife. Even if she was dog-ugly, he could still get a lot of work and some offspring out of a young one!

He assumed that if those crooked surfmen had gotten into the salvaged trunk, no doubt they would have kept anything of value. The few dealings he'd had with them had convinced Silas that these men would have helped themselves to part of it at least, as anyone would have! But maybe, just maybe the girl had some of the gold.

As he rode out there, he tried to recall the exact conversation that he'd had with that station keeper, what's-his-name. The man mentioned a chest but did not say that any trunks or gold had been recovered. But then again, he did *not* say that nothing had been recovered. So perhaps old Saltman's belongings were somewhere in the station, inventoried and waiting to be retrieved by relatives or sold at auction. Silas grinned and rubbed his hands together.

The old nag that he had hired eventually delivered him to Tilly's home, right where the man told him it would be. Silas was tired of this sandy, desolate place and anxious to get back to Charleston. His town-home there would have to be sold if he couldn't get hold of some ready cash soon; the plantation was bleeding money and in need of a large infusion. It was prime bottomland, but the days of Reconstruction were leaving the Southern landowners struggling to keep their heads above water, much less turn a profit.

Simon Beaufort and his father had lied, stolen, cheated, murdered and maneuvered enough to keep his family's land during and after the war. Having been 'unfit' for duty as a soldier (due to a convenient leg injury he claimed), Silas was able to stay at home during the fighting, work the farm, hide anything valuable from the pilfering Yankees, and shoot any stragglers that showed their face around the place.

His father had hired the meanest man he could find to be his slave overseer and the man managed to keep a few negroes from bolting after the war, telling them that they had nowhere to go anyway and threatening to kill their children if they tried to leave. Since his father's death, things had been going Silas' way and if he had anything to say about it, that's the way things would go on from here! War or no war, Silas Beaufort was coming out on top!

He got off the horse, stretched and walked up to knock on the front door. Sarah was out back with the stock at the time, but Tilly was inside cooking when she heard the knock. Wiping her hands, she looked out the window and saw the unfamiliar horse. She opened the door and found a strange man standing there, hat in hand. He fit the description Erv had given them perfectly.

"Yes?" she asked cautiously.

"Would you happen to be Mrs. Downs, Ma'am?" he asked politely.

She stood tall and crossed her arms. "And who would be wanting to know?"

He laid his hand over his chest. "Oh, do forgive me, please!" Silas put on his very best Southern Gentleman. "My name is Silas Beaufort; I'm from Charleston, South Carolina, and have come here to call on a Miss Sarah Fletcher. And you would be Mrs. Downs? Do I have the right house?" He smiled ever so pleasantly.

"What business do you have with Miss Fletcher?"

He looked down and twisted his hat a bit, sounding emotional. "Well, you might say that she and I are family – or as near as can be. I have just recently discovered that she survived that awful shipwreck that killed my dear friends the Saltmans, God rest their souls," he said, lowering his chin for a few long, respectful seconds in a typically Southern show of respect for the dead. "It was a tragedy indeed, but my heart was lightened beyond words when I found out that my dear Sarah had survived!"

Tilly said, "I did not know the Saltman family, but I am sure that you are correct in saying that it was a tragedy. Especially for Sarah, who had been like a daughter to them."

His head popped up. "But she was not actually blood kin, was she?" he asked. "I mean, you know, she was like a daughter but not really a daughter," he backpedaled quickly. "That is what I was told…"

Keeping her arms crossed, Tilly leaned forward. "Mr. …Beaufort, is it?"

He nodded and smiled.

"I don't see that any of this is your business, Mr. Beaufort. Sarah is under my protection and anything that you have to say to her you will say to me as well." Tilly stared him down.

Silas had expected to be invited in by now; the odd thought occurred to him that things here might prove to be a little more difficult than he had anticipated. *But then, he did love a challenge, especially with women.* "Of course, Ma'am, of course. But would the sweet young thing be anywhere about so that we can, the three of us, have a little chat?" He looked around hopefully.

Tilly came outside, closing the door behind her. "Follow me."

She stepped off the porch and he followed her. "Of course, Ma'am... This is a fine place you've got here, right nice property. I also understand that you are a poor widow woman. It is indeed impressive that you can keep it up as well as you have, being alone and all..." he rattled on as they walked around the back. The more he talked, the more Tilly got the measure of the man.

They made their way out to the barn and Tilly stood outside, calling to Sarah. No way was she going to let this man in to get a look at any of her assets, livestock or otherwise.

"Yes, Tilly?" Sarah said, coming out and closing the door behind her. When she saw the man standing beside Tilly, she stopped short.

"Oh, Miss Fletcher, it is so good to see you!" Silas said, stepping forward. "At long last we meet. I have looked forward with anticipation to this moment with all my heart!" He gave her his most tender smile, which was still a fearsome looking thing at best.

Sarah looked to Tilly. Tilly said, "Sarah Fletcher, this is Mr. Silas Beaufort from Charleston, South Carolina. He has come here to call on you." She gave the younger woman a knowing look. Silas headed in Sarah's directions, his arms out.

Sarah held out her hands, palms out, lifted her chin and said, "Stop right there! You are a stranger to me, Mr. Beaufort. I have no business with you, Sir, so you can leave now." She gave him a dismissive look and began to turn back toward the barn.

Silas was surprised that this young thing had a backbone; he smiled inwardly thinking that it was going to be great fun breaking this girl's spirit. "Forgive me please, Miss Fletcher, but I do believe that we have some business together. Your guardian, Mr. Amos Saltman, and I entered into some binding legal contracts before he passed away, which do involve you. Would you please give me the chance to explain the details to you?" He glanced back toward the porch.

She stopped and turned around. "Explain, then, and please make it brief," Sarah said, putting her hands on her hips. Tilly smothered a laugh.

"Can we not sit for a moment in the shade on the porch? I am dreadfully tired after my long boat trip and then the horse ride to get out here. It was a dreadfully long trek, and I am tired and thirsty…"

Sarah looked questioningly at Tilly; Tilly nodded to Sarah.

Sarah said, "With Mrs. Down's permission we can use the porch for a few minutes, I suppose. But we both have work to do and do not need to be resting at this time of day. You will be quick about it," she added, turning to walk toward the porch.

Beaufort hurried to catch up with the young woman. Still reeking of syrupy Southern manners he said, "You are *much* lovelier than I was led to believe, Sarah, and – "

Sarah stopped short and glared at him. "I have *not* given you permission to call me by my given name, Sir, and you are a stranger to me! That is a terribly forward, ill-mannered thing to do!"

He stood, shocked for a moment. *This girl might even need some beatings to tame that tongue of hers!* "Please do forgive me, Miss Fletcher, I forgot myself there for a moment. It is simply that I feel as if we know one another because Amos spoke of you in his letters in such detail…"

She stood her ground. "Well, he spoke not at all of you! All I was told is that we were going to South Carolina to inspect a man's property and if – *I said if* – he approved of *everything*, we would consider moving there. I was under the impression that no formal contracts – business or otherwise – had yet been signed."

Tilly grinned, standing behind them. They had 'rehearsed' this confrontation and Sarah was doing better with her performance than she could have hoped. *Between the two of them, maybe they could dispatch this fool and be done with him,* she decided.

Silas extended his hand toward the porch, ignoring Sarah's comment. "Shall we?"

Once settled, he looked at Tilly. "Would it be too terribly much for me to beg you for a drink, Mrs. Downs? As I said, I am powerful thirsty!"

Without answering, Tilly got up and went inside. She quickly poured him a glass of water from this morning's kettle.

Silas scooted his chair closer to Sarah's, puffed out his chest and looked into her eyes, smiling and heaving a long, silly sigh. "I could not have asked God for a better woman to share my life with than you. You are obviously a fine girl; one so lovely that any man would be proud to call you his – "

"*His what?*" Tilly interrupted, stepping out onto the porch and handing him a glass.

Startled to see her back so quickly, he jumped a bit, but then gratefully took the glass from her hand. *This woman must be faster than a racehorse!* He took a sip and almost spit it out, *warm water!* He managed to give Tilly a quick smile and a 'thank you' through gritted teeth.

"Well, Mrs. Downs, I was just going to mention to Miss Sarah – uh, Miss Fletcher, excuse me – that she and I are happily and legally engaged. Amos Saltman and I signed a legal marriage contract some weeks before their ship left port. He might not have mentioned it to the girl so as not to get her little hopes up." He nodded obsequiously.

"He knew that I am a man of means; I have a large plantation as well as a fine town home in Charleston, and no doubt thought that informing her of my proposal would be a jim-dandy surprise once she saw all of that for herself! After all, there are not many girls who wouldn't give their right arm to be so well set up with a fine husband these days." He bounced his head side to side on his neck to make his point. Both of the women simply stared at him.

He was beginning to run out of patience with this lot. The old lady was definitely not coming with them when he left with this girl! "I am sure that you also see the advantages in a marriage like that yourself, Mrs. Downs, being a widow yourself, and I know that you want what is best for the g – for Miss Fletcher."

Tilly took a chair on the other side of Sarah, straightened her skirts slowly, looked him in the face and said, "Miss Fletcher is of legal age now, Sir, so any contract that was made on her behalf cannot possibly be legally binding at this time. Especially something as questionable as a marriage contract made without her knowledge or consent!"

Sarah nodded her head. "That is my thinking as well. So, as I said, you can be on your way back to South Carolina as soon as you have finished your water."

Beaufort's ears turned red with the effort he was making to hold his temper; he had been blindsided by that statement. While he had discussed marriage to the girl with Saltman, no actual contract had been made...but these women did not know that now, did they?

He decided that at this point it was still worth trying to catch these flies with honey, not vinegar. "You do not understand what you are saying, dear girl, you are little more than a child and have no knowledge of legal proceedings. This marriage contract," he said, tapping his jacket pocket to make the papers inside rattle, "was made on the basis of honor and mutual trust and cannot be overturned lightly. Amos Saltman was your legal guardian when he signed it, was he not?"

Sarah faltered. He had in fact been her guardian for all practical purposes.

Tilly interrupted, "Yes, the Saltman family had generously cared for and supported Miss Fletcher, but they were not her **legal guardians**. There is no paperwork."

He thought fast. "I was told differently. No doubt there will be a copy of that guardianship document in the Courthouse at Columbus, Ohio. Getting a copy will be a simple matter settled by telegraph," he said, barely hiding his anger behind a frightening show of teeth. "As her legal guardian, Saltman was fully empowered to make binding contracts on her behalf and she is duty-bound to fulfill those obligations."

Sarah stood up, and he promptly rose from his chair. "Then, Mr. Beaufort, no doubt you will have little trouble producing such a document, along with all the other appropriate documentation to support your case. There is a North Carolina circuit judge that comes along from time to time and he will be glad to examine your proof and hear your claims when he gets here. But for now, you must leave!" Tilly stood up beside her, nodding.

"You stubborn little..." Beaufort composed himself before continuing. "I will indeed be back with all that paperwork. And you will be ready to go to South Carolina with me on that same day, missy! And you will bring everything that survived the shipwreck that is yours or was Amos Saltman's – because all of it belongs to me legally – or it will *when we marry*. I wish you ladies a good day and look forward to seeing you again soon."

He tipped his hat, quickly walked down the steps and over to the old swaybacked horse, mounted and got on his way.

As soon as Beaufort was out of sight, Sarah fell back into her chair, trembling. "Oh my, that was worse than I thought it would be! How did it go, do you think, Tilly?"

She shook her head slowly. "Well, between the two of us he found out right quick that he was not dealing with a couple of ninnies. But what he said about legal guardianship troubles me some; do you know if Mr. Saltman was indeed your legal guardian?"

Sarah shrugged. "I cannot say. Before Mother died, she told me repeatedly that the Saltmans were taking responsibility for me and would take good care of me. Whether they got her to sign a legal document or not – I simply do not know, no one ever mentioned it to me." She got a frightened look on her face. "What if there is a legal guardianship paper and he gets his hands on it? Would I have to go with him?"

Tilly moved her mouth around, but then shook her head. "We must find a way around it if that comes up. *We will find a way*, don't worry, child." She put her arms around Sarah, hugging her tightly. "There is no way in hell that I'm letting that man take you off!"

Sarah looked at her with big eyes. "Tilly!"

Tilly grinned and they both broke up laughing. They decided that it was now time to visit the Life Saving Station and get some advice from the men.

Chapter 29

This time the four of them sat around the table at the Station as Tilly and Sarah recounted the details of Silas Beaufort's visit. Erv interrupted briefly to ask a few salient questions, and Josiah sat, mumbling unintelligible words and shifting around uncomfortably.

When the telling was finished, they looked from one to the other; Erv was the first to speak. "Well, even though you got rid of him, we have to assume that he will be back… Now that he has seen our fair Sarah, he would come back for her even if he gets nothing else. As of right now, he knows nothing about the chest, the documents, or the gold, and hopefully he will simply reconsider and change his mind, deciding that dealing with the two of you is more trouble than it is worth!" He grinned at them.

"Erv," Josiah said, "did you inventory that chest after the shipwreck? Did you list it as salvage?"

Erv swallowed. "Well, yes, I did but I did not list everything that was in it, I simply said 'personal items' as 'contents of chest'. And I made the note that it had been given to Miss Sarah Fletcher, who was under the guardianship of the Saltmans, so it was legally her property."

Josiah rubbed his face. "Oh, no! He can get his hands on a copy of that inventory list if he has not already done so. What if he wants to use the legal system to contest Sarah's right to it?"

Tilly moaned. "If he can prove the Saltmans' legal guardianship along with a legally binding marriage contract, then there is a remote chance that he could win any legal case he might bring. Powerful men tend to take the sides of other powerful men. We have a new judge riding this circuit that none of us has met yet; he *could be* the kind of man who wouldn't think twice of a woman being some man's property. We simply do not know what kind of man this judge will turn out to be."

Large tears came up into Sarah's eyes and she fought to hold them back. "I cannot... I will not marry that man! He is horrid! And he is old enough to be my grandfather!"

Tilly reached over and took Sarah into her arms to comfort her as the sobs began. "And you will not have to, dear, if any of us have breath left in our bodies!" She looked at the two men and raised an eyebrow.

"Of course!" Erv said.

"That will happen only over my dead body!" Josiah said fiercely, jumping up from the chair and rushing out the door.

Erv looked at Tilly and whispered, "Tis not *his* dead body that I concern myself with! There is no telling what that young man might do. We simply cannot let that happen!"

Tilly nodded and hugged Sarah even tighter.

Chapter 30

Nags Head, North Carolina

Silas Beaufort sat in a dockside bar, picking at what little food was offered there. *Disgusting stuff it is, too, always some kind of fish, fish, fish!* He could hardly wait to get back to his home in South Carolina where the women knew how to cook ham and cornbread!

He fumed as he thought about those two hussies on Hatteras who had so brazenly stood up to him and then dismissed him. *Those two will get what's coming to them!* he thought as he chewed angrily and downed his third shot of some locally made whiskey. A man walked into the place, grabbed a chair and slid it up close to Silas' table, but remained standing.

"What do you want?" Silas asked, glaring up at the man.

The stranger looked Beaufort up and down, rubbing his chin.

"Well?" Beaufort demanded.

"Would you be the man from South Carolina who has the interests down Hatteras way?"

Silas eyed him. "Who wants to know?"

The man smiled and Silas noticed that he seemed to have most all of his teeth, unusual as that was. Actually now that he noticed, the fellow was fairly well dressed for these seaside ports, where many of the people went barefoot and often shirtless. He looked like he might be... important somehow.

"In a place like this, few strangers have any secrets, sir. I believe that you and I might be able to help each other out in a business kind of way that could be mutually beneficial," the man said.

"My name is Jedidiah Walker, and I assume, Sir, that you are Mr. Beaufort?" He extended his hand.

Silas hesitantly shook the man's hand, becoming more and more curious. "Yes, I am Silas Beaufort. What can you possibly do for me in this godforsaken place, Mr. Jedidiah Walker?" As he spoke, he noticed that the room had become quiet and all eyes were on the two of them. It was true, then, that these people had already found out his business.

"Well, Sir, I am a lawyer and I understand that you are in need of some legal assistance..."

Silas looked him over. *Who was this man?* He did seem like a lawyer, with his decent-looking clothes, a clean hat and his obvious education. And he was right – Silas did need a lawyer! But the kind of man Silas needed had to be someone who would be legally... well, *flexible* for want of a better word.

"Well, sit down then. Stand you for a drink, Walker?" he asked. When the man nodded, Silas called the owner over and ordered what he asked for. Walker turned the chair around and sat on it backward, giving a casual yet confident impression.

"Now then, it's like this," Silas began, lowering his voice so that the whole dad-blamed nosey bar couldn't hear the conversation. "There is a young woman down in Hatteras Island who was promised to me in marriage by a man from Ohio who was to be my business partner. They were all shipwrecked on Hatteras on the way down and that girl was the only survivor. She is living there with a widow woman and they will have nuthin' to do with me."

Walker nodded and encouraged him to go on.

Silas said, "I told her that Saltman, the man who had promised her to me, had agreed to not only invest all his assets in my plantation outside Charleston, but also to let me have her as a wife. My first two wives are dead, you see, and I need to get me a young gal to get me some offspring."

Jed Walker made a strange face but then said, "Go on."

"And... well, I know for a fact that Saltman was traveling with gold, lots of it. He had sold out his business and properties up north and was comin' down to investigate my property before he paid me his half. I got hold of a guv'ment record that says that a chest that had belonged to the Saltmans was salvaged from the shipwreck. Everything else got scavenged by the local good-for-nuthins who live off what washes up on shore!" He spat on the floor, shaking his head.

Jed Walker's eyes shifted around the room. "You are in a bar full of that particular kind of people, Beaufort, so please keep your voice down."

"Oh... oh! Of course." Silas cleared his throat. "Well, anyway, they gave the Saltman's chest to the girl, so I am thinking that she has all of Saltman's gold that was recovered. Nobody has mentioned any gold, but I would bet my bottom dollar that it was there on the ship with him, and a chest like that would be the safest place to store it. So I need to get the girl – who is stubbornly refusin' to even discuss it – so that I can get the gold. And, the girl, well she is a young, lively thing and I want her pretty bad, too," he added as an afterthought, wiggling his eyebrows.

Walker tried hard to get past the manner of this man to see if any possible profit might be had out of the deal. "Do you have signed documents with Mr. Saltman about the business partnership and the marriage contract?"

Silas shifted about uneasily in his chair. "Well, not exactly. I have all our correspondence with the details of our proposed partnership – "

"*Proposed partnership*? You mean that Saltman never even signed a business agreement with you?"

"Well, he was going to! But the fool would not turn loose of his gold or make any kind of commitment until he looked the place over for himself. It was as good as done, but we had not actually even met face-to-face. It was all handled by correspondence."

Walker thought it over. "How did you come in contact with him to begin with?"

"I put an advertisement in a paper up north, looking for a partner in my farming business. I figured somebody up that way might have some money, there sure ain't much to be had down South these days. He answered the listing, we corresponded for some time, and then he made the decision to move down." Silas shrugged. "Maybe he needed to get away, I don't know. All I know is that he was coming and he had gold – lots of it!"

"How old is this young woman?"

"Just turned eighteen, I believe."

"Was Saltman her legal guardian, so that he could make a contract in her behalf for her marriage?"

"I, uh… I don't know exactly. And that is where the problems come in; there is no written marriage contract, it was something we discussed – once. But if the girl's got the chest, then I need the girl to get the chest!"

Walker grunted.

Silas said, "I thought that perhaps I would just go on down to Hatteras, stake my claims and everybody would believe me. But the men at the Life Saving Station – the ones who saved the girl – as well as the old lady she is living with, they would have nuthin' to do with it without seeing legal papers, which I ain't got." Silas put out his hand, palm up. "So there you have it! It was all to be mine, but now I cannot prove any of it!" He downed the remainder of his whiskey.

Jed Walker put his arms across the back of the chair he was sitting on, crossed his hands, leaned his chin down onto his hands and considered the situation. Finally, he said, "A marriage contract made like that, now that her legal guardian has deceased and she is of legal age, well it would be left up to the discretion of a judge to decide which way it goes." He shook his head. "And from my experience, Mr. Beaufort, any good judge is going to side with the girl because she will be seen as the victim in all of this."

"Her?! I, Suh, am the victim in all of this!"

"From your point of view only, Mr. Beaufort. In my professional opinion, you have not a leg to stand on legally."

Silas slammed his fist down on the table, but Walker didn't flinch. "That is not the kind of legal advice I am about to pay for, Suh!"

Walker cleared his throat. "So…exactly what kind of advice *would* you be willing to pay for?" He desperately needed money and would do just about anything to get enough to make it out west.

Beaufort looked him over. Maybe the man could find a way around some of this mess and help him out. "The kind that would git me what I want, of course!"

Walker stood up, turned the chair back around, straightened his jacket and said, "Let me give this some more thought. I will be back here tomorrow morning if you care to meet me. I have an idea or two, but it will take some devious thinking and serious planning, if you've a mind to do that kind of thing. Let us say, nine o'clock tomorrow?"

Devious – I like the sound of that! Silas thought. "If you can present me with a workable plan, Walker, then I would be willing to pay you real good for your efforts. And the more devious the better, I say."

Jed Walker smiled and Silas saw then that the guy had 'slick' written all over him. "Yes, you definitely will pay me well, Mr. Beaufort, *very well*. Until tomorrow." He tipped his hat and turned, walking out of the place.

Silas' mood lifted considerably and he ordered another drink.

Chapter 31

The following morning the two men breakfasted together at the same place. After commiserating about the lack of civilization on the Outer Banks, Silas asked about his main concern regarding Walker. "So just what is a fancy lawyer like you doing down in this place with all these fishermen and pirates, anyway?" He waved his hand around at the other patrons dismissively.

Jed laughed and took a drink of his bitter coffee. "Actually, I am down this way on a – well, let us call it a sabbatical – because my business up around Washington required that I make a hasty departure to... a place where nobody could find me," he said, shrugging. "Does that bother you at all, Beaufort?"

Silas shook his head slowly and grinned. "Not at all. In fact, I believe that the two of us could rub along quite well together. So, what was this plan that you spoke of? I am all ears, lawyer-man."

Walker pushed his empty plate aside and glanced in both directions cautiously. "I arrived here a few days ago, just looking for a place to lay low where nobody knew me, and when I came into town several of the locals asked me if I was the new Circuit Judge, who's supposed to come through soon. I must look like a lawyer, I suppose..." He shrugged.

Silas guffawed and then said, "Sorry. Yes, you do, bless your heart." He snickered again.

Walker ignored the little jab and went on. "So I made a few inquiries about this judge that is due soon and found out that nobody around here knows him. His name is Lewis Tolbert; he is the new Circuit Judge for all of eastern North Carolina, and that is a large territory. Nobody knows when he is expected; I suppose that in places like this they simply show up from time to time, take care of whatever legal business has been saved for them, and then move along." He rolled his eyes and shook his head at the loose arrangement.

"So?" Beaufort held out both hands.

"So..." Walker tapped the tabletop with his finger as he made each point. "...you could go back to the island with some very legal-looking papers that I can make up for you. Then I could come down Hatteras way and pose as this Judge Tolbert that nobody knows, and we act like we have never met. You could present me with your legal case. I could then utter some judicial-sounding terms and rule in your favor. You would get the girl and the gold. Nobody would question the ruling of a Circuit Judge." He clasped his fingers together and rested his hands on the table.

Silas brightened and worked his mouth around while he thought. "That might just work! You *are* a devious thinker, Mr. Walker! We could get in and get out and then disappear before anybody was the wiser. I would marry the girl and her gold would be mine, and nobody could do anything about it, even if later on they found out the documents were forged!" He laughed loudly.

The bartender seemed to appear from nowhere and asked, "Can I get you men some more coffee?"

"No! Git!" Silas answered, waving him away.

Jed Walker returned his attention to Beaufort and gave him his best shifty-looking smile; Silas loved the look of that charming, calculated grin.

Silas sobered suddenly and leaned forward. "And what would your price be for doing me this excessively good turn?"

Walker smiled again – only this time Silas didn't care for the evil smile at all. "Half the gold, whatever the girl got." Beaufort leaned back, crossing his arms over his chest.

"Half!" Silas exploded, pounding the table again. "Ain't no way in hell you will get half, Walker!"

"Quiet down, Silas," Walker said, looking around at the surprised faces of the other patrons scattered about. He leaned forward. "We are in the negotiation stage at this point. If not half, then forty percent..."

Silas put his palms on the table and drew back. "Huh, not on your life! If there is as much gold as I think there is, you will get... *twenty* percent of it and that will last you a good long time. You can git far away from Washington and your 'friends' up there."

Jed Walker rubbed his chin. "Tell you what, Silas. Because I like you so much, I will settle for twenty-five percent. But that is my final offer. And without me, I *guarantee* that you will not get a penny – or the girl." He let the offer hang in the air and then made to stand up.

"Wait, wait," Silas said, motioning him to sit back down. "Alright, twenty-five percent it is. But after we are done, you will simply disappear and never be seen in these parts again, right?"

"Absolutely. I do not care to spend any more time in this place than I absolutely must! Everything here reeks of fish guts!" He sniffed the air and made a face.

"Done, then." Silas extended his hand.

Walker got that grin – the one that Silas didn't care for – on his face again. "Done. Let's work out the details."

Chapter 32

A few days later Walker had the official-looking documents finished, and together they laid out all the details of their plan. Silas hired a boat and went back to Hatteras Island. He made his way straight to the Life Saving Station, believing that when the government men saw the 'documentation' that they would not give him any more trouble.

Erv, who was most unhappy to see the man again, looked it over and then passed it to Josiah, who studied it carefully. They shared a glance. Things did not look good for Sarah – the paperwork he'd brought seemed to be in order and to legally back up all of Beaufort's claims.

"Of course, you will still have to go in front of a judge with these documents," Erv said, tapping the papers. "We will do nothing without a legal representative of the State of North Carolina making sure that everything is done legally."

Silas snorted. "Yeah. I'll just bet that nothing ever happens around here without official guv'ment approval..."

Josiah threw the papers back at him. "*This* will certainly not happen without a Judge enforcing it, Beaufort! So you can crawl back into whatever hole you came out of until such time as we receive a visit from the new Circuit Judge – and nobody knows when that will be!" He looked smug.

Silas smiled innocently. "As a matter of fact, when I was up in the northern Banks I heard that the new judge is comin' out this way soon, a matter of days I was told. I sent a telegram that day requesting that he come here to Hatteras straightaway to settle this matter so that I could get on home to South Carolina and back to my farm. He telegraphed back that he would be here soon. I will find a place to stay until he arrives and *then* we shall see what we shall see, Gentlemen!"

He stacked his paperwork up and shoved it into the leather carrying case. "I will give ya'll the privilege of telling the ladies that I am back. Until then..." He walked out of the station house, strutting and humming.

Erv raised an eyebrow and looked at Josiah. "So the new judge is on his way? Mighty convenient how that worked out for him, don't you think?"

Josiah nodded. "Well, when the judge comes, hopefully he will be a fair man and be willing to listen to Sarah's side of the story. And she is over eighteen now, so maybe he will rule that she is free to decide for herself who she is to marry."

"Hmmm...." Erv said, tapping the tabletop with his index finger. "I believe that 'tis time for me to make a quick trip to the northern Banks and...get some more supplies, Josiah."

He gave him a questioning look. "But we just got a delivery, not - "

"Yes, 'tis time, do not argue with me, Boy!" Erv said firmly.

Josiah couldn't understand why Erv would run off at a time like this. "You will be right back, won't you? Sarah is going to need us if all of this does come before that judge."

Erv nodded, stood up and said as he walked away, "I shall return as soon as possible. In the meantime, you are in charge. The weather looks good; you should have no problems." Erv went upstairs to throw a few things into a bag.

Josiah looked puzzled and also disappointed. It wasn't like Erv to run away from a fight like that, but the man usually knew what he was doing, so no doubt he would be back in time to help Sarah, if she needed him.

Chapter 33

Three days later, 'Judge Lewis Tolbert' got off the boat at the port of Hatteras and made his way to the nicest room for rent available in the nearby village. The local folks (who cared not at all for sheriffs or lawyers or judges) did not give him the respectful welcome he had expected, but he nonetheless went about setting up his 'court,' to begin proceedings on the following morning.

Word was sent up to the Life Saving Station that Sarah's case would be heard the following day. Josiah was still waiting for Erv to return; it was not like him to be long away from the Station. But no doubt he was fine and had encountered some unforeseen Life Saving business to attend to. So Josiah made his way to Tilly's house and informed the women of where they needed to go the next day.

"Will Erv be there?" Sarah asked nervously. "You told us that Beaufort had some official-looking documents and I would feel so much better if Erv could attend the court and be there for me…"

Josiah hung his head. "Erv had to go north to get some supplies, but he said he would be right back. That was three days ago. Surely he will return sometime today. And yes, both of us will be there for you, you know that we will. In fact, we will hitch up the dray to a wagon and come and get you to take you there."

Tilly smiled and patted the young man's hand. "You are a good man, Josiah, and it is considerate of you to escort us. We certainly do appreciate it."

"I would not be anywhere else, Ma'am. If that Beaufort thinks that he can force Sarah into doing anything that she does not want to do, then judge or no judge, he will have to go through me!"

Sarah smiled at him and took his other hand. He squeezed it and refused to let it go for a long time.

Not long after sunrise the next morning, he drove up in the wagon, got out and knocked on Tilly's front door.

Tilly answered. "Come on in, Josiah, we were having a bit of breakfast. Did you eat yet?" she said, ushering him into the kitchen.

"Eat? Me?" Josiah looked confused. "Oh my gosh, I do believe that I forgot to eat breakfast this morning!" he said, looking embarrassed. For the first time he could remember, food had been the last thing on the young man's mind. *This might be love*, he thought to himself.

"Then you must come in and let us take care of that, dear boy. We have a long day ahead of us, and ham, biscuits and gravy is just the thing!" She looked around. "Where is Erv, is he not with you?"

Josiah shook his head worriedly. "He should have been back by now. But I left word where we would be, so he may come down to Hat'tras village if he gets back in time…"

Sarah also looked troubled; she, too, had wanted the strong, reliable presence of Erv Brophy for moral support at court.

The village schoolhouse was rearranged for the day to serve as a makeshift courtroom. The teacher's desk had been cleared of everything, and the students' desks were grouped together in several rows for the crowd that was expected. A few chairs had been placed in front, on the judge's right and left, for the 'prosecution' and the 'defense', such as it was.

Roughly twenty people had heard the judge was in town and gathered to tend to legal matters, both large and small. And more than a few were there simply because it was the most exciting thing happening in Hatteras for months. Jed Walker came in and took his seat, posing as Judge Lewis Tolbert. Earlier that morning he had been shown only a modicum of hospitality by these queer folks; he would be glad to be out of here. And he could tell that the residents of Hatteras Island would certainly be happy to see the back of him. But he was here, and it was time to get on with it...

Three cases had been scheduled before Sarah's; two were small property disputes and one was an actual murder case. Jed Walker's eyes lit up when he saw the docket; he had wanted to be a judge for years, and now he would be getting his chance. He smiled; *may as well dispense a little justice as part of the show!* That would make things look all the more legitimate.

Wilbur Todd, the Mayor of Hatteras, called for quiet. "Court's about to start! The Honorable Judge Lewis Tolbert presiding! Ya'll set down and shut up!"

Morning light streamed in through the windows as everyone who had stood up now took their seats. Walker looked around the assembled group, giving them his best judgmental look. "Circuit Court is now in session. Let us begin," he said with authority.

"Where's your gavel, judge?" a man in the crowd quipped. "You got one, don't you? Judges is supposed to have gavels, I thought." Several guffaws were heard. Walker stood up and glared ominously at the man.

"I... left it at my last posting, and that comment had better be the last disruption in my court today, or I shall be seeing cases of contempt when the scheduled cases have been heard. Does everyone here understand that?" He slammed his large hand down on the desk, startling everyone. He looked at the man who had spoken. "Will my fist be enough of a gavel for you, sir?"

The room suddenly grew quiet, and only some foot-shuffling could be heard. "Now," he said, taking his seat again, "let us get right to it. First case, please." He looked to his left.

The mayor of Hatteras Village stood and took his place as acting bailiff and coordinator. "First up, Your Honor, is the case of Jeb Squinley versus Edward Squinley."

"A family squabble?" Walker asked. There was considerable titter from the audience. Walker grinned; he was fitting nicely into this role of judge. He was suddenly hit by a flash of insight. *Might be that I could get away with posing as a judge out west once this is over and I have got a little money in my pocket…*

The Mayor's words brought him back to reality. "No, Your Honor, tis a bit of a property squabble, actually. Jeb here says that his cousin Ed is running livestock on his property and that he ain't got no right to be doing that. Ed has been taking a few from the herd as payment now and again, and Jeb says he ain't got no right to be doing *that*. So that is what this whole kerfuffle is about."

Walker nodded and said, "We shall have it all settled soon enough, Mayor. Let me hear the evidence, please. You first," he said as he pointed to the first 'wronged' man.

Thus began the first two cases, which Walker eventually got all sorted out and the proper amount of justice dispensed. He left the Squinley cousin's situation as it was, ruling that a cow or sheep now and then seemed like fair payment for grazing rights. If Ed didn't want Jeb's animals on his land, he could put up a fence. If Jeb didn't like paying Ed, with or without his knowledge, then he'd better keep the stock off his cousin's land. Neither of them was very happy with the verdict, but they walked out together and headed over to the bar to work out the details.

The next case was more serious; Frank Woodard had been accused of stealing Thomas Goody's fishing boat. Around here, that kind of thing could lead to violence; but in this case, there was simply no proof. The accused thief had been gone for a week or two round about the time the boat was stolen; he'd come back and had some unexpected cash in his hands, which he said he had bragged about winning while playing poker at some fish camp somewhere; he couldn't exactly recall where because he had been drinking pretty heavy at the time.

The boat's owner assumed that the stolen boat had been taken and sold by Woodard. He was accused of taking it in the dead of night, but no witnesses had actually seen him take it. Goody had made efforts to locate his boat as far north as Currituck and as far south as Ocracoke, but nobody knew anything about it. Still, he had put two and two together and accused the newly flush Frank Woodard, who naturally claimed innocence.

After hearing everything they both had to say, 'Judge Tolbert' said, "Well, boys, this is the way I see it. *Somebody* stole that boat. While we've got no proof Frank Woodard is guilty here, we have what we in the legal profession call 'reasonable doubt.' But − on the other hand, Mr. Woodard's story about where he got the money sounds a little bit too convenient to me... Now, Mr. Woodard, how much money did you say that you won at the gambling table in that fishing camp?"

Frank Woodard puffed out his chest. "Over five hundred dollars, Your Honor!"

"And what was your stake to start with?"

Frank hemmed and hawed. "Uh... maybe fifty dollars?"

Someone yelled out, "And where did the likes of *you* git fifty dollars, Frank?"

Walker smiled but called for quiet. He turned back to Woodard. "You must be quite a poker player, Sir!"

Woodard nodded enthusiastically. "Oh, yes I am, Your Honor. Everybody around these parts knows how lucky and how good I am!"

A few guffaws and comments from the audience were heard.

Walker tilted his head and studied the accused man, who was looking confident and pleased; after all, there was no real *proof* that he had stolen the boat. Goody, the boat's owner, stood a few feet away from him, looking quite angry and more than a little disappointed that he had left this important matter in the hands of the 'law.' His idea had been to beat the money out of Woodard.

'Judge' Walker stared at both of them and rubbed his chin. "Well, my judgement in this case is this: Since you came by the money gambling and did not have to work for it, Mr. Woodard, you can give half of it – two hundred fifty dollars – to your fine neighbor Mr. Goody so that he can begin to get himself another boat to make a living for himself and his family."

The audience erupted in laughter and then applauded.

Woodard looked like he might protest for a moment, then hung his head and nodded. Goody, while not happy that Frank didn't go to jail, was mollified by getting the sum of two hundred fifty dollars; after all, his boat wasn't worth much more than that.

Walker oversaw the exchange of money and the two men left. He was quite proud of himself, all in all, and began to think that he was much like wise king Solomon, who had ordered the baby split in half to find out who its real mother was. His was probably the best justice these people had seen in years, especially out here in this hind-end of civilization. *I shall make a most impressive judge out west*, he thought to himself as he rolled that idea around in his head. *And I will give them swift and fair justice.*

Chapter 34

Next up was the murder case. Olley Proud had shot Zach Russell dead after he found out that Zach had been carrying on with his wife. Olly freely admitted that, yes he had shot him, and he would do it again if need be. His poor wife sat, cowed with fear, in the back of the schoolroom. He turned to her and said that if it *did* happen again, he might even add beating her to death to his list of crimes.

Testimony about the dead man was heard, and evidently that Russell fellow had messed about with more than one wife in this small village, but nobody had done anything about it before, short of a little beating and a lot of threatening. The man was a real lowlife to hear it told, a good-for-nothing Romeo-type who lived off of women he could bamboozle into taking care of him.

Walker gave everybody a break for some lunch while he thought that one over. It was murder, no doubt about that; Olley Proud had admittedly shot the man in the back. But...

When court resumed that afternoon, word had gotten out and everybody in town tried to get into the schoolhouse to hear what the judge would say about this case. So far, the opinion of the community was somewhat divided; some said that this new judge was fair and just; others said that he ignored the law. It certainly made for some spirited lunchtime conversation.

"Judge" Jed Walker entered into the packed room and order was called. He sat down and looked around the room, studying the crowd that had come. He had played to crowds all his career as a lawyer, and he could read this one pretty well. *They will like what I have to say*, he told himself. *Naturally, for my words are wise and fair and just.*

He cleared his throat and adopted his best official tone. "Murder is not a crime to be taken lightly. We cannot have people go around shooting each other for petty reasons, that is for sure. And in this case, the accused has freely admitted shooting the victim in the back, so it is a clear cut case of murder."

The crowd murmured its agreement, heads nodding. The people were holding their breath awaiting his decision.

Walker held up one finger. "However, sometimes we have what we in the legal profession call 'extenuating circumstances,' and that is what we have in this case."

Several people in the audience looked at each other, clearly confused by the legal jargon.

Walker noticed this. "What *that* means folks, is that sometimes there is a good reason for a person doing what they have done."

"Oh.... ahh...." was heard in a generally low tone.

"And it looks to me like not a soul in this village seemed to think very much of this rabble-rouser that was killed. His only character reference was his mamma – nobody but his mamma cared that he was shot dead – and let's face it folks, every mamma loves their boys even if they are good-for-nothing scoundrels. Right?"

The crowd broke up in laughter. Walker sat a little taller and smiled. *This was all going quite well! He would make a fine judge out west!*

"Some people, excuse me, Mrs. Russell, for saying so," he added, nodding toward the dead man's mother, "well, some people *just need killin'* for the good of the community." The poor old lady covered her face with her hands and began to wail. The Mayor quickly saw to it that she was removed from the room.

Order now restored, the 'Judge' went on. "So, in this particular case, I am applying the Law of Extenuating Circumstances. And since the boy is dead and gone and nothing can be done about *that* at this point, I am going to rule that the accused," he said, pointing to the man standing in front of him, "is not guilty by reason of extenuating circumstances."

Before the crowd could react, he raised his voice loudly and added, "But now – and all ya'll listen to this part – don't you people be thinking that you can do whatever you like down here and get away with murder if you don't like somebody. All of you need to be making a good reputation with your neighbors so that if your turn comes, there will be somebody besides your mamma to stand up as a character reference for you!"

The crowd erupted in shouts, applause and laughter. Walker was having the time of his life, basking in the glow of open admiration. He let the revelry go on a bit before calling the court back to order. The accused man walked to the back of the room, grabbed his wife roughly by the arm, turned to wave to the crowd, and was gone.

Silas Beaufort had sat through all of this, wondering why Walker was putting on such a show. Now he understood – whatever the 'Judge' ruled at this point would be heartily supported by this crowd. This scoundrel was proving to be worth his share of the gold!

Chapter 35

When Sarah's case was announced, Tilly and Josiah came forward with her. Erv had still not arrived, and had evidently been held up; they were all sorry for that because they needed his moral support and strength.

"Mr., er... Beaufort, is it?" he asked, looking around as if he had no idea who was who in this town.

"Here, Your Honor," Silas spoke up, standing in front of Walker and to his left. "That would be me, Silas Beaufort of Charleston, South Carolina." He held his hat in his hands and nodded.

"Fine, then, and let's see... Miss Sarah Fletcher?" he said, looking toward the three standing to his right.

"Yes, Your Honor, that is me," Sarah said, lifting her chin. "Sarah Fletcher of... well, currently of Hat'tras Island."

The judge nodded. "Let me see the paperwork, Mr. Beaufort, if you have any?" He extended his hand, looking a bit weary.

Beaufort stepped forward and handed a sheaf of papers to Walker, who examined them at length. He looked toward Sarah's group. "Do you have any paperwork for me, Miss Fletcher?"

She stepped forward and handed him the correspondence that she had recovered from the chest, a little yellowed and wrinkled, but still legible.

"A bit the worse for wear, isn't it?" he asked her as he handled them.

"Yes, Sir, the paperwork was sealed in an almost waterproof chest that belonged to the Saltmans and I am afraid that it has suffered a bit of water damage. It was recovered the next day on the beach by a surfman and the Keeper of Little Kinnakeet Station, Erv Brophy, who later declared the chest to be my property after he identified its owner."

"Why *your* property, Miss Fletcher? You are not of the Saltman family, are you?" Walker asked innocently.

"Your Honor, she was adopted by the family and was the closest relative that we could find, so Erv figured it belonged to her," Josiah put it.

"And you are?" Walker asked Josiah.

"Josiah Miller, Your Honor, Second-in-Command at the Little Kinnakeet Life Saving Station."

"Well, Mr. Miller, if I need anything from you I will ask, but from this point forward, if I ask Miss Fletcher a question, you will let her be doing the answering, do you understand?" he said sternly.

"Yes, Your Honor," Josiah answered respectfully.

"Good. So where is the Station Keeper, why is he not here today?" Walker asked, looking around. Nobody answered.

"Are you asking me this time, Your Honor?" Josiah said. More tittering was heard from the audience.

"Yes, of course, Mr. Miller, who else would I be asking?" Walker slammed his fist down on the desk and pointed toward the crowd. "Any more racket from all ya'll and I shall have this room cleared!"

The crowd settled down; they wanted to stay. There had not been entertainment this good in Hatteras in recent memory, and nobody wanted to miss a minute of it.

"Captain Brophy was called out of town on business, I expected him back already..." Josiah said.

Walker waved his hand. "Let's get on with it, then, I would like to take the last boat out of here and back to civilization before this day is over. What are your claims, Mr. Beaufort?"

Silas stepped forward a little. "Miss Fletcher here was promised in marriage to me while she was under the guardianship of Mr. Saltman. Saltman and me also had business arrangements, and as you can see from the paperwork, we were to be business partners. Alas, he perished before we could complete the business, but it is my position that Miss Fletcher is still legally bound by that marriage contract that you have in your hand, there. She says she is not. We need you to settle that for us." He stepped back.

Walker looked at Sarah. "I notice that the marriage contract was signed several months ago. How old are you now, Miss Fletcher?"

"I am over eighteen, Your Honor," she said, looking pleased to say so.

"And how old were you when Mr. Saltman entered into this marriage contract on your behalf?"

"He did nothing *on my behalf*, I mean to say, that he did not mention the contract to me at all, your Honor. But I only just turned eighteen a few weeks before our ship was wrecked, so I was probably seventeen when – or if – he made that arrangement." She looked to Josiah for support.

Walker shuffled some more papers. While this was no murder case, it was getting interesting and the locals were all playing close attention. Walker studied one of the papers. "I see here that Amos Saltman was declared your legal guardian some time ago. Where are your parents, Miss Fletcher?"

Sarah was surprised. *"He was?* I did not know that, no one ever told me, Your Honor. You see, my father died when I was little and my mother passed away more than two years ago…"

The 'Judge' nodded. "No doubt your dear departed mother thought that the Saltmans would take good care of you or she would never have signed this document of guardianship." He waved an official looking piece of paper in the air. He turned to Silas. "You say this document is a copy that you secured from Columbus, Ohio, Mr. Beaufort?"

"Yes, sir, I telegraphed and they sent it to me straightaway," Silas said, turning to give the three of them a smug look.

Walker shuffled the papers for a few more minutes. "Well, everything looks to be in order. Is the marriage contract the only thing that is at issue in this case?" He looked between the groups in front of him.

"No, Your Honor," Silas said.

Walker looked up. "Well what else is it, then; I don't have all day to do this, you know, Beaufort!"

"Well, there is the little matter of the Saltman's recovered property, Your Honor..." Silas said. "Not that there was much of it, but I believe that whatever there happens to be in the chest concerns me and the arrangements we had made together." He had no intention of drawing any attention to the contents of the chest. If indeed there was gold inside, he did not want any of these scroungey-looking fishermen to get wind of it. He wanted to get it out of here safe and sound, with no fuss.

"Just some paperwork in the chest, then? That all?" Walker asked.

"A few family items, and some jewelry, as well..." Sarah said. Josiah gave her a look.

"Jewelry? What is the worth of the jewelry?" Walker asked, suddenly more than mildly interested. "What kind of jewelry?"

"They never said nuthin' about no jewelry, Your Honor," Silas bellowed. "They been trying to hide the contents of that chest from me all along!"

Walker looked at Sarah, who looked to Tilly.

"Your Honor, may I speak?" Tilly asked.

"Who in hell are you and what have you got to do with all of this?" Walker asked. He was clearing becoming agitated with all these unforeseen details.

"Mrs. Tilly Downs, Sir. Miss Fletcher came to live with me after the terrible ordeal of being shipwrecked. She and I have become quite close."

"Well, that's fine and dandy. And exactly what do you know about this jewelry?"

"Well, Your Honor, I looked at it and found it to be mostly costume jewelry, none of it worth much money. Mrs. Saltman was wearing her gold wedding band when she died, evidently. So it is my opinion that the value of all of the jewelry in the chest could not be any more than five dollars, Sir."

Jed Walker exhaled heavily. "Five dollars, huh? Well, that don't matter a'tall that I can see one way or the other." He looked at Sarah. "Back to this marriage contract, then. Miss Fletcher, were you under the protection of Amos Saltman and his wife for many years?"

Sarah nodded. "Almost as far back as I can remember, Your Honor. They were like a second set of parents to me. My mother worked for them, and later I did as well. We all lived in the same house. They were excessively kind to me."

"So do you not feel that you owe them something in return for everything that they did for you over the years of your young life?" he asked.

Sarah hung her head. "I only wish that I could pay them back in some way, Your Honor, for all the good things they did. But alas, they are gone now, together with their children, and I can do nothing for any of them."

Walker got a smug look on his face and that slick smile appeared. "Oh, I believe that *you can*, Miss Fletcher."

Sarah looked up, confused. "What can a living person possibly do for the dead, Your Honor?"

He leaned forward and lowered his voice. "You can honor the memory of the man who raised you like his own daughter by making good on this marriage contract that he so thoughtfully provided for you!" he said, waving that particular 'document' in the air.

"You are, as their adopted daughter, legally obligated to do so, in my opinion!" He set the document down on the desktop. "Either you are their legal heir and entitled to anything of theirs, or you are not! If you are an heir, then you are also legally bound by this contract!"

Sarah gasped and grabbed Tilly's hand. "No, Your Honor, no, I am now of an age that I can make legal decisions for myself and I do not want to marry that man!" she said, pointing toward Silas Beaufort. "You cannot make me!" She immediately covered her mouth after the outburst.

A lot of stirring around, whispering and foot shuffling was going on in the audience, but they wanted to see the end of this, so they kept it fairly quiet.

Walker sat back and crossed his arms. "Oh, I believe that I can, Miss Fletcher. I am the Honorable Lewis Tolbert, a Circuit Court Judge officially empowered by the State of North Carolina; and this being my district, *what I say here goes*, legally speaking. And it is my judgement today that you are legally bound to marry Mr. Silas Beaufort. *Both legally and morally*, because your adopted father was concerned enough for your future to provide you with a husband who is a gentleman and a man of property and means besides! Many a young woman would be thrilled to have such a husband!"

He slammed his fist down once again and said in a loud voice, "Miss Sarah Fletcher is hereby ordered to fulfill the marriage contract that was entered into on her behalf by her legal guardian, Amos

Saltman. Miss Fletcher, according to the laws of North Carolina, you and all your property will be the possession of Mr. Beaufort as soon as the marriage is officiated. That is how the law works, Miss Fletcher. My best wishes for your happiness." He shuffled and stacked the papers. "Court adjourned!"

"Yee haw!" Silas said, flailing his arms around. "Thank you, Judge!"

Walker pointed to Beaufort and said sternly, "Do not thank me yet, Mr. Beaufort. All I can see that you are getting here is an old trunk of some kind and a brash, mouthy woman. You may live to regret my ruling this day."

"No, no, no!" Sarah cried, throwing herself into the arms of Josiah for protection. Beaufort moved in their direction and Josiah sent him a threatening glare.

Silas looked toward the judge. "Your Honor?" he said, pointing toward the large human barricade that stood between him and his prize.

The 'Judge' stood up. "Mr. Miller, please remove your hands from Miss Fletcher. I have the authority to issue marriage licenses and perform marriages, and I am doing both right now. I shall marry the two of them and settle all this before I leave today!"

The entire courtroom, previously stunned into silence, was then thrown into confusion. Even though the locals did not care much for the shipwrecked girl recently washed up onto their shores, they would not take kindly to one of their highly respected surfmen being bullied about, judge or no judge.

Walker shouted. "Everybody get out of here except the ones who are getting married. Now!"

Chaos erupted.

Chapter 36

Suddenly the schoolhouse door was thrown open. They all looked around to see the silhouettes of two men standing in the doorway with the sun to their back. After blinking a bit, most of them recognized Erv Brophy, if not the man beside him.

Erv walked to the front of the large room and turned to face the crowd. "You lot settle down, now, I got something important to say," he shouted over the commotion.

The locals were ecstatic. This was high drama indeed and these fishermen would see that this story would be told in every bar up and down the Eastern Seaboard before the month was out!

Erv looked to Josiah. "What's happening here?"

Josiah filled him in quickly, and Erv turned again toward the crowd, his back still to Jed Walker, who stood up and flew into a fit and said, "What is the meaning of this? This is my courtroom and I'll have the hide of any man who dares to come in here and disrupt – "

Erv whirled around to face him and shouted, "Oh, I do not think that you will be having anybody's hide this day, *Your Honor*. You sit down and shut up!" he said, pointing toward Walker.

"Arrest that man, Mayor!" Walker yelled at the mayor, who stood there with his mouth hanging open.

All eyes turned to Mayor Wilbur Todd. He shifted uneasily. After all, this was supposed to be a day that made him look good as he did his official duty, and he didn't want to spoil it by offending anyone. The Mayor swallowed hard, thought fast and then spoke.

"Well, Your Honor, to tell the truth, I do not know you from Adam, but I do know this man," he said, pointing toward Erv. "And Keeper Brophy is one of the most respected men in this county. He and his crew have saved many a life on these treacherous waters, and if Erv's got somethin' to say, the good people of Hat'tras Island are going to hear him out!"

Walker fumed but shut up.

The crowd roared. Nothing like a local man giving a high-falutin' fancy-talkin' judge a good set-down!

Erv called for quiet. "My friends and neighbors," he began, locking his thumbs under the suspenders holding up his best pair of pants, "what we got here is not justice. 'Tis the awful ridiculous *injustice* of an evil man posing as an angel sent from god!"

The laughter that followed urged Erv into his best official stance and he continued, pointing toward Walker. "This so-called *judge* here is not a judge at all! He is no more than a washed up lawyer from Washington who is pretending to be a judge! And I found out that he is wanted by the law himself up that way to face some serious charges of his own!"

"How dare you!" Walker shouted back. "I shall see you in a federal jail for making false accusations like that! You have nothing but your own word, and we can all clearly see which side of this case you are on – you have no right to say a word in my courtroom, and I'll see you – "

"Aye, and I will be seeing *you* in the jail because I have proof!" Erv declared, and smiled. Silence descended on the courtroom. Heads kept sliding back and forth to keep up with what all the principal players were saying.

The people of Hatteras Island had fought for the Confederacy, but they now considered themselves to be Americans and were proud of their country. On the one hand, they trusted Keeper Erv Brophy, but on the other hand the authority of a government-empowered judge was nothing to be taken lightly, either. They settled in for the thrilling resolution of this matter.

Erv took advantage of the lull. "This man," he said, pulling on the arm of the fellow he had come in with, "is Mr. Everett Cook. He runs the place where all of you stop and get a drink or a bite to eat when you're up in Nags Head. His place is called The Gull's Gizzard; you all be knowing the place!"

Beaufort and Walker turned to look the man over and both of them swallowed hard; he was the barkeep in the place where they'd met and made their deal.

Heads began to bob up and down as recognition of the man drifted through the audience. The ones who did not know Mr. Cook knew the head-bobbers, so pretty soon the consensus was that Cook knew what he was talking about and should indeed be heard. "*Let him talk!*" and "*What do you know, Cook?*" could be heard coming from the assembled group.

Cook stepped forward for his moment to shine. "Ladies and gents of Hat'tras Island," he began. More head-bobbing started – *at least this man knew how to say the name of the island right!* "When Silas Beaufort first come to Nags Head, he told me his story and I believed everything he said. After all, a man's got a natural right to some things, and both salvage and women fall into that category!"

The two-thirds of the audience that was male made sounds of agreement with Cook's first statement. The women present hesitated; salvage was one thing, but not a one of them liked this Beaufort character and they all felt pretty sorry for Sarah. None of them would want to marry that smarmy little fellow, rich or not.

Cook went on. "When Beaufort come back up from his first trip to Hat'tras, he told me how he had been cheated out of what was his and that he was going to get some proof and come back down and git it. I figgered if he could prove 'twas his, then that was that and he was entitled to what was his own."

"And he has proof!" Walker said, waving those same pages around in the air.

Cook turned and stared Walker down, then resumed talking to the crowd. "Don't know about that there, but I do know this: when this here feller what's claimin' to be the judge come to town, he didn't say nothin' bout bein' no kind of lawman nor judge. Just said he was passin' through. And when the two of 'em set down together," he said motioning between Walker and Beaufort, "I heard enough that night to know that both of 'em was up to no good!"

He leaned forward as if to share a secret. "Well, I listened more close-like when they got together the next mornin' and heard 'em talkin' bout comin' down here and pullin' the wool over ya'lls eyes. But then, 'tweren't none of my business. I do keep myself out of other people's business, ya'll know that!" He looked around and several of the men nodded in agreement, happy to be reassured that Cook kept secrets, for he had also seen a few of them from time to time taking care of their shady business in his establishment.

"Listen carefully to him, now!" Erv said to the people, who were beginning to talk among themselves.

Cook took a deep breath. "Well, I heard that un," he said, pointing toward Walker, "tell this un", pointing toward Beaufort, "that he was some kinda washed up lawyer in trouble, but that he could make ignorant fools like ya'll believe he was a judge, and he would help Beaufort out of his mess by writin' up some official lookin' pieces of paper to support his side and then rule in his favor at court if he paid him enough!" He put his hands on his hips and nodded briskly. "Yep, he said that!"

The courtroom erupted. Cook waved his arms and called for silence. "So then, when Station Keeper Brophy come 'round lookin' for anybody who knew anything 'bout the new judge, I told him what I had overheard. He wired the gov'ment in Raleigh and they wired us back that the real Judge Tolbert was down in Greensboro and wouldn't be out here with us no time soon!"

The crowd gasped collectively; they had been hoodwinked by a crooked lawyer!

Erv piped up. "And after a few more inquiries, I discovered that this man's name is Jed Walker and he himself is a man on the run from the law up in Washington! 'Tis true!"

The Mayor shouted, "We have been taken for fools! What kind of skullduggery is this?" He turned to face Walker.

Josiah rushed around the teacher's desk and grabbed Walker by the lapels. "Why you good for nothing, lowdown, swindler!" he said and he drew back his fist. The crowd gasped again and held their breath. Walker didn't stand a chance against those arms that could row a surfboat out past three sets of breakers in stormy weather. Josiah landed one well-placed punch and the 'Judge' went down like a sack of potatoes.

The rest of the men rushed toward Beaufort and grabbed him. "I say we lynch 'em both!" one man said, and a murmur of agreement ran through the crowd. "Lynch 'em!" became the cry of the whole lot of them.

Chapter 37

"Wait, wait, now just a minute!" Erv cut in. "Ya'll settle down, now!" After the crowd quieted a bit, he went on. "There will be no hanging done here today. While the two of 'em have tried to bamboozle and swindle all of us and abduct our poor, dear, Sarah, none of that is a hanging offense, I don't reckon. We need to save 'em over till the real judge comes and let him have a crack at 'em!"

That was not a popular opinion; the men of Hatteras Island had been called fools, then bamboozled into believing that Walker was a real judge, and these two scoundrels had almost gotten away with it. They were unanimously of the opinion that it was high time for some fisherman's justice!

The mayor took charge of the fracas, instructed that the two men be locked up in the shed outside the school, and told everybody to cool off and go home, he would handle it. Several large men drug the limp body of Walker and the struggling form of Beaufort out the back door. Some of the crowd gathered outside the schoolhouse, talking things over.

The mayor signaled to one of the men who was escorting Walker and Beaufort out. He walked over and whispered to the man, "Hank, listen. Shut the door good and stand a man outside the shed to make sure that nobody gets out – or in – and then come round to my place tonight after everything settles down. Ya got that?"

Hank nodded and headed out to make sure that it was done.

The mayor walked over to the disgruntled group of men and ladies and gave them a big grin. "Everybody here alright with what's been done?" he asked.

Sarah, Tilly and Erv all voiced their agreement. Josiah just stared at him. The rest of the crowd hemmed and hawed, but didn't put up too much of a fuss. They had, after all, been looking forward to a good hangin'.

The mayor slapped Erv on the back. "You have done a fine service for your community this day, Keeper Brophy, and have averted a terrible miscarriage of justice at the same time. Well done, Sir, well done! Let me stand you all for a drink down at the Port Tavern, yes?" he said to the assembled crowd.

The men all nodded and even Tilly smiled in agreement. The mayor offered his arm to Sarah, apologizing profusely for putting her in jeopardy. As they walked out the schoolhouse door, he stood on the top step and addressed the crowd assembled outside.

"Now, all ya'll remember that today justice was done here in Hat'tras, and when election day rolls around don't forget that it was Mayor Wilbur Todd who made it happen!" He waved happily to the crowd, who by now were cheering for Erv and Sarah. *Never let a good opportunity to take credit for something go to waste,* that was the mayor's motto.

A man cried out, "But Mayor, what about them three other cases that the fake judge ruled on? What about them?"

The rotund man paused and thought for a moment. "Well, them other three verdicts sounded like pretty good justice to me, so I reckon we will let them stand as-is. That alright with all ya'll?"

After a short period of discussion, shouts of approval rose from the crowd. The mayor nodded, waved and walked on. A single man caught up with him and whispered, "But what about the Squinley cousins, Wilbur? Both of them got drunk as a skunk, passed out and already got hauled back home..."

The mayor smiled and his eyes twinkled. "Pass the word around that nobody tells them boys any different, let 'em believe that he was a real judge."

"But they're bound to find out sooner or later!"

"Well, when that happens, they'll be right back where they started, won't they, and no better or worse off than before. It won't make no difference anyhow, you know them Squinleys are gonna do what they want to do, anyway, judge or no judge!"

The man nodded. "Yep, I reckon you're right about that, Wilbur. Let's go on and get us a drink – you say you're buying?"

"I will buy you one, after than you're on your own!" the mayor said, and took a laughing Sarah by the arm and toward the bar. The entire village gathered to celebrate a monumental day that would not soon be forgotten in the small fishing village of Hatteras.

A little after dark, the Mayor was visited at home by Hank, the man who had put people on watch over the two men in the shed. He pulled Hank inside after looking around. Shutting the door behind him, the Mayor whispered, "Now this is what I want you to do..."

When he finished, the man nodded, grinned and asked, "What time?"

"Not before midnight. And between now and then, go and let a few of my men – you know which ones I'm talking about – know what's goin' on. But only a few, and nobody else, you got that?"

"Uh-huh, got it. How bad you want it to be?"

The Mayor thought it over. "Well, that South Carolina fella owns a plantation and somebody might cause a ruckus if he disappeared... but that crooked lawyer fella, ya'll give him whatever justice you think he is due, just don't tell me what you do. And this will be the last we ever talk about this, you understand?"

"Yes, Mr. Mayor," the man said, grinning. "We'll take care of it."

Chapter 38

After a brief celebration, but before things got too rowdy, Josiah drove the ladies back home. He helped them down from the wagon and Tilly asked him to come inside.

"I best be gettin' back to the station, Tilly, but I thank you all the same. Erv and me – we shall come back soon and check on the two of you to make sure those scoundrels haven't come back around."

Tilly stepped up on the porch and laughed. "Well, Josiah, I don't reckon that we will be seeing either one of those two around these parts again. I feel sure that the new judge will take care of them good and proper!"

"Thank you, Josiah," Sarah said, taking his hand. "You have been such a good friend through all of this – I do not know how we would have made it without you..."

"No worry, there, Sarah, nobody will be messing with you while I – that is, all of us surfmen are around!"

She smiled up at him and squeezed his hand. "That makes me feel so safe!"

Josiah felt a compelling urge to scoop her up in his arms and keep her safe forever. Instead, he grinned, nodded and tipped his cap. "Yes, Ma'am." He drove off in the wagon, Sarah watching until he rounded the corner.

After settling in, Tilly called Sarah over for a chat. "So now your future is entirely up to you, Dear. What do you feel inclined to do?"

Sarah's big eyes looked lost. "I...I do not know, Tilly. The past few days I have been so concerned about being taken away from you – and from all my friends here... One thing that I have come to realize is that I have no desire to leave this island. You, Erv and Josiah, in fact everyone, have become like family to me. So, I suppose I had better give it some thought now that things have settled down..."

"Do you really think that you could live out here, so far away from the life in town that you were used to?"

Sarah tilted her head and thought about it. "This place – the peace, the beauty of it, even the rough wildness – well, it makes me feel like life is full of potential. I never had the adventurous desire to move way out west and start a life there, but here I have a sense of hopefulness; I want to see how this island develops, how life here unfolds for all these hardy folks who have made it their home. Do you think that the local people will accept a girl like me with no family?"

"If what happened today is any indication, they have already taken you into their hearts. I imagine that every man on this island feels a strong need to protect you from anything that might harm you!"

"And the women?"

She laughed. "Well, you know how women are. At first they thought that you were just too pretty for your own good; but now, when they hear about what almost happened to you, they will take you in as well, I believe. I do not foresee you having any problems, if you decide to stay here. Once you get married and settle down, they will think of you as one of 'us'."

Sarah blushed and looked down. "How will I know when I am ready to get married, do you think, Tilly?"

The older woman patted her on the arm gently. "I suspect that by the time some man asks you, you will have pretty much figured it out."

Chapter 39

Over at the Station, all the men were celebrating and giving Erv his well-deserved pats on the back. Josiah said, "I had no idea what you were up to, Captain, but you sure saved the day!"

Erv shook his head. "Just doing what was right, Josiah. That is a surfman's job, you know." He grinned. "Looks like our Sarah is free now to marry whoever she pleases!" The men cheered.

Josiah paced the floor. "In that case, I'm gonna go ask her right now, Captain! Can I take the horse?"

Erv looked concerned, but nodded. "You know that this cannot happen right away, don't you? I mean, your place here, your future... Unless you mean to leave the service and start somewhere else?"

Josiah shook his head. "I know, it can't happen for a while... But just knowing that Sarah's mine – well, that's all I want!" He took off running, and Erv laughed.

When Sarah saw Josiah coming back, she went out onto the porch, waving at him. "Is everything alright?" she asked as he came closer.

Josiah nodded. "Fine and dandy. I just need to talk to you. Can I come in for a little bit?" he asked shyly.

"Of course. Tilly and I were having tea; you'll join us?"

Josiah agreed. Upon taking a seat, he cleared his throat and said, "You know, Sarah, I was not going to let Beaufort marry you. I was even willing to marry you myself to stop that from happening!" He looked so proud.

"Oh, my…" Tilly said, her eyes wide.

Sarah stared at him, saying nothing for several long moments. "What did you just say?" she asked.

"I said," he went on, smiling at her, "that I was going to marry you myself to keep that man from taking you off." He grinned at her.

"You were going to…do what?" Sarah asked, shaking her head.

He sat up straight. "Well, you see, it's like this," he answered, "I was going to throw you over my shoulder in the courtroom and run you over to the docks. I have got a friend who's the captain of a schooner that's docked there. He had agreed to marry us in a hurry. That way, you would already *be married*, and Beaufort could not lay any kind of claim to you!" He crossed his arms and grinned at her. "See? It was the perfect plan!"

Sarah looked at Tilly, who simply rolled her eyes. Then Sarah stood up and walked around the kitchen slowly, running her hands over the tops of the chairs as she circled the table. Finally, she turned to Josiah and said, "You were going to carry me off – just like that?"

He grinned and nodded.

"Were you not even going to bother to ask me first?" she demanded.

"Well…I just figured that…"

"That what?!"

"That you would rather marry me than old Beaufort?" he asked, losing a bit of his momentum.

She put her palms on the table and leaned toward him. "If – and I mean if – I *ever* get married," she said firmly, "it will be to a man who has courted me and then asked me proper-like. Not to some idiot who throws me over his shoulder and runs off with me!" Sarah turned around, fled the room and ran upstairs.

After a few moments, Tilly patted his hand and said, "That didn't go too well, did it?"

Josiah sat, dumbfounded, scratching his head. "What did I say wrong? I offered to get her out of a bad situation by marrying her myself! What was wrong with that?"

Tilly sat at the table across from him. "Josiah, I know that you meant that to be…special. But, all in all, that was the worst marriage proposal I ever heard of!"

He rubbed his face. "But I love her, Tilly, and I want to marry her someday…"

Tilly sat back in her chair and thought. "Well, then, you need a plan, son. You need to understand that a girl wants to be courted, made to feel special, and then you need to get down on one knee and make her feel like she's the most beautiful woman in the world when you ask her to be your wife."

He shook his head sadly. "I never get it right! The feelings in my heart try to come out of my mouth and they get all messed up! I wind up saying the wrong, stupid thing every time I talk to her! She'll never have me, now!" The big lug looked like he might cry.

"Now, now, do not give up hope just yet. I know for a fact that she cares very much for you, Josiah, and it would not surprise me in the least that if you ask her again – after some time and courting – she might just jump into your arms and cover your face with kisses!"

He began to look a bit hopeful. "Really? Do you think so?"

Tilly nodded. "Right now, the best thing that you can do is go on back to the station. Then pick some flowers in a few days, come back and apologize for your awkward marriage proposal, and ask permission to court her properly. Then, after some time passes and you have convinced her that you love her and need her, you can ask her again – and I'll help you plan it out the next time. How does that sound?"

He lit up. "Oh, thank you, Tilly! I am a real idiot when it comes to saying things to her…will it ever get better, do you think?"

She patted his hand. "I expect so, Josiah. But you might want to think things over a little bit more before the words roll out of your big mouth."

He nodded. "I'll try…"

Chapter 40

a few months later...

Tilly and Erv sat together on the porch of her house, she on the swing and he in a rocking chair, enjoying the sunset together.

"Did you hear about that body they found last month?" he asked.

She turned to him. "No! What body?"

"Well, it seems that some man's body – or part of one, at least, washed up on the soundside of Hat'tras a couple of weeks ago."

"Oh, that's awful!" she said. "Do they know who it was?"

He grinned.. "Well, 'tis a bit of a mystery because it seems the gators gold hold of it – at least that's what Mayor Todd told me – and it had been floating in the water for some time, which made it, well, a wee bit difficult to recognize..." Tilly made a face.

Erv went on, "But most of the top half of the body was there, so they took an educated guess. No local men are missing, and from the clothes he was wearing and what they could make out of the face, the fellows who found him said it appeared to be that crooked lawyer fellow who posed as the Judge..."

She turned and looked at him, shocked. His lopsided grin softened her shock and she began to sputter, then laugh. They laughed together and not another word was said about *that*.

"Well, whatever happened to Silas Beaufort, did he go back to South Carolina? We haven't heard a word about him..." she asked.

"Uh...well, Wilbur Todd told me that after they locked him up in the shed – and they said he put up a godawful fight about that and was badly beaten as a result – that he was set loose the next day and put on a boat headed south. Wilbur did say that he was in pretty bad shape when they threw him on the boat. He probably made it home eventually, but nobody has heard a thing. I doubt we'll ever be seeing the likes of him again around here."

Tilly tilted her head. "Did the Hat'tras boys rough him up?"

Erv shrugged. "Wilbur did seem to know more about it than he let on, but if you remember, Tilly, the crowd was going to hang both of them on the spot that day and he would not let them do that. So it could have been worse...for Beaufort, anyhow..."

Tilly said, "Let's not mention this to Sarah."

"Agreed."

They sat peacefully together as only dear friends of many years can. Erv cleared his throat. "Now that Josiah and Sarah are to be married, and he is taking over as Keeper of the station, Tilly, I will be retiring next month, you know..."

"Yes, Erv, I know."

He exhaled heavily. "Well, there is something that's been on my mind for some time now and I need to talk to you about it."

"Go ahead," she said, staring off into the sunset.

"Well, it's like this, Tilly...after I leave the Life Saving Service, I will be needing a place to live..."

She neither spoke nor looked at him.

He had been looking for a little encouragement, but none was forthcoming. "So...do you think that maybe I could rent out Sarah's old room, now that they have built that new house over by the Station and are getting married and all? We, the two of us, could live here together and keep one another company, Lass."

- 194 -

Her head snapped around. "Rent Sarah's room? Did you say 'rent the room', Erv Brophy!?"

He swallowed hard and nodded. "Unless you think that people might talk, and in that case we could go ahead and make it official."

"Make what official, Erv Brophy?" She squinted her eyes at him.

He took off his cap and rubbed his head. "You're not making this easy, woman! You know what I am talking about!"

She sat with her arms crossed over her chest and stared at him.

"I'm too old to get down on one knee, Tilly, I might not be able to get back up!" He gave her a pleading look.

They stared at one another until Tilly burst out laughing. Erv was not sure how to handle that response, but eventually her laughter became contagious, and both of them wound up doubling over, wiping tears from their eyes.

Finally, Tilly smiled at him and said, "Good Lord, Erv, you are even worse at proposing marriage than Josiah Miller was!"

He grinned. "But you got the idea, right? So, will you marry me, Tilly? You know that I have loved you for years and years! When I asked you the first time years back, you turned me down flat. But we don't have that much time left in life, so why don't we spend it together?"

She straightened her skirts and looked around. "I always said that I would never marry again, Erv, you know that..."

He grunted, then a thought struck him. "Tilly, you know the motto of the Life Saving Service, 'You have to go out, but you don't have to come back'?"

"Yes, I've heard it enough times and worried over you enough times!"

"Well, every time we went out on that surfboat to save people, we truly did not know if we would come back alive. But that did not stop us from taking the chance to do something good. And it worked out fine, we always came back and lives were saved!"

She nodded.

"Well, marriage is a lot like that – you got to take a chance to be happy. If you just set on the shore waiting, before you know it, your chance to do good, to save your own life is gone and you can't go back and undo it. Marrying me 'twould be nothing like being married to that other man was!"

She smiled and reached over, taking his hand. "I know that, Erv, truly I do." She shook her head and gave him a look of love. "I am not very good at eating my own words, but in this case, I do believe that I will do just that. Perhaps, Erv Brophy, I will marry you – but..."

He sat up straight and smiled. "But? But what?"

She pointed a finger at him. "You have to court me proper-like, at least for a little while. And then you can ask me and I will *probably* say 'yes.' Can you do that?"

He looked flummoxed. "I don't know, Tilly, I never courted a woman before. I don't reckon that I rightly know how..."

"Ask Josiah, he will tell you how it is done," she said smugly.

"Ask Josiah?" The very thought of going to a younger man for that kind of advice seemed to paralyze him. But then he softened and said, "I suppose I could do that. It sure worked for him when he asked Sarah last week. The girl said 'yes' before he even got the words all the way out of his mouth!"

Tilly nodded. "He knows just what to do. He had a good teacher."

He took her hand in his, squeezed it and they sat in silence watching the sun descend on the waters of the Sound.

"Oh, Erv," she said after a few minutes, "did I ever tell you about my late husband Edward's will?" she asked.

He scratched his head. "No, I don't believe you mentioned it, Tilly. Did he have one?"

She nodded. "Yes. And in it he stated that he wanted to be buried with all his money in the casket with him."

"He never!" Erv said, leaning forward. "What a black-hearted son of a – "

Tilly held up a finger. "Well, the minister who spoke words over him and me were the only two people who saw it. The law normally gives all property to a surviving widow, so everybody just assumed that is what happened. But before he was buried, I showed the handwritten will to the minister. My conscience was bothering me a little, I guess, because I knew that was what Edward had wanted." She looked away.

"What did the minister think of that, Tilly?"

She smiled. "Well, he looked at it, thought about it for a long time, and then gave me some excellent advice."

"What did he say?"

"He told me to write Edward a check for the full amount and put it in the casket with him. So that's what I did." She grinned at Erv, who almost fell out of his chair laughing.

Chapter 41

Seven years later

"Josiah, that daughter of yours is going to be the death of me!" Sarah said, throwing her face against his chest.

He wrapped his arms around his little wife. "Now, now, Dear, she's just a little girl…"

Sarah looked up at his weathered face; she loved this man so much! "Well, even at five years of age, she has a mind of her own. Her little brother has been as easy as pie, but since he was born, Tilly acts like a brat! She will listen to nothing I say! What am I going to do with her?"

He hugged her tight. "I shall talk to her. You know that she is an awful lot like me – things just pop out of her mouth and she doesn't think a thing about it! She's also a lot like Big Tilly, hardheaded and independent. Maybe our next little girl will be more like you…all sweet and easy."

Sarah got a look of longing on her face. "If I survive to have another one… but then this girl might just be the death of me!"

He laughed and set her aside. "I will go outside and talk to her, Lass. She will listen to me." He nodded and headed out the door.

I doubt it seriously, but you go ahead and try, Sarah thought.

Josiah called his daughter, and she ran to him, throwing herself into his arms. "Papa! Papa! Come and look at the sandcastle I'm building!"

He set her down and bent over to talk to her. "In a minute, Little T. Right now Papa wants to talk to you about how you upset Mother. Did you talk back to her?"

Little Tilly shuffled her foot around in the sand. "I...I guess so..." She glanced up, a perturbed look on her little face. "But, Papa, Mother is very, very bossy!"

Josiah smothered a grin. "Yes, she can be at times. But she is your mother, and it is her job to be your boss; in fact, that is every mother's job, to boss around their little ones. It keeps you out of trouble if you listen to her." He looked into her eyes. "Will you promise Papa that you will try to do better and mind your mother from now on?"

Little Tilly scrunched up her face. "I guess so." She gave him a pitiful look. "But Papa, it is *so* hard to be good!"

"I know, I know, Little T, but all of us must try. Your mother loves you very much – "

"More than she loves little brother?"

"*Just as much* as she loves little brother. She will love all of her children just the same. But you will always be special to her, do you know why?"

Little Tilly shook her head.

"Because you were our very first baby! We prayed for you to come along and you came to us, just like a little angel!"

She beamed. "So I am special, Papa?"

He nodded and hugged her tight. "Yes you are, my Little T, very, very special!"

PART 3

HEALING FROM THE INSIDE OUT

Chapter 42

HATTERAS ISLAND, MODERN DAY

Hannah tucked her feet up under her, laid the old, tattered journal down on the coffee table, and stared at it. For the past three hours she'd read this woman's most intimate thoughts and feelings, her entire life story in an outlined, condensed version. Running through Hannah's mind were questions about many of the details that were not spelled out – like what happened to many of those people mentioned – all kinds of things that she would likely never learn the answers to.

It had been like a movie playing in her head, this woman's life. Yet never had the writer mentioned her own name. Her husband's name, Josiah, her children's names, other people, but never her own name, just 'me', 'I' or 'we' when referring to herself.

And yet, it had to be the same woman that her dear neighbor Finis' grandmother Tilly had told him the stories about: Granny T's mother, Finis' grandmother, the woman who had been shipwrecked on Hatteras Island, the sole survivor of a terrible accident at sea. The one who had been fished out of the water by the man who would later become her husband...

This had to be Finis' great-grandmother's journal!

She fingered the red velvet bag, moth eaten and deteriorating. Which baby had worn those shoes? All of them, perhaps, including Granny T? In the very bottom of the bag she felt something else. Opening the mouth of the bag up wide, she looked inside, searching for whatever the small item was. She spotted something metal and drew it out. It was a twenty-dollar gold piece!

It *had* to be part of the gold the writer had mentioned in her diary - the gold that was given to her after the shipwreck — that had belonged to the family who was bringing her down to South Carolina! She fingered it gently, rubbing it with her thumb to shine it up. Dated 1868! Imagine what it must be worth today!

If old Mr. Midgett had ever come up here and gone through all of that junk and found this, he'd never have sold the house to her! At least, not with the chest in it! She laughed out loud. Finis was going to love reading this journal - his family heritage, many of his questions answered about his great-grandparents, the mysterious 'family treasure', and personal details about the brave young surfman who would become his great-grandfather!

It was an intimate glimpse into the thoughts and feelings of a young woman who had lost everyone she cared about, was alone and afraid, but who came into the care of new friends who saved her life and then helped her to build a new one...A timeless story that revealed the depth of human emotion, uncovering the best and worst of both ordinary and extraordinary people.

Tears came into Hannah's eyes; as she had been reading, something felt intimately familiar about the woman's story, and now she realized what it was. *This was her story, in a way.*

She had also lost everyone she loved, and was now alone in a place that was harsh and wild - and yet at the same time welcoming and nurturing for her. She had begun to build a new family for herself, beginning with Smiley and that lovable old curmudgeon Finis Turnbull, and now her dear friend Phil, the veterinarian.

Finis had to know about this; she was going over to see him! Hannah came out of her fog, recognizing the sound of Smiley whining and scratching at the door. He'd been patient, but now he was letting her know that some things cannot be ignored forever.

While engrossed in the journal, she had totally forgotten about the bad weather, about Smiley, about her own problems, about...everything else. As she opened the door to let him out, she realized that the sleet had stopped. It was still a cold, windy, cloudy day, but to Hannah it didn't feel that way; it was a lovely day, a happy life, new and full of promise.

She walked into the kitchen, her tummy letting her know that it was long past time to eat. Hannah fixed herself a bowl of soup and as she ate, she thought about her late husband Mark. How she had loved him, needed him and felt complete with him. He had been her whole life, her reason for living. What would he want her to do with her life now?

If the situation were reversed - if it had been Hannah who died and Mark was the survivor - what would she have wanted for him? The little round crackers floated on top of her soup, popping up every time she'd push one of them under with her spoon. She smiled. *That's what I'd want for him, to be like those crackers, to keep coming back up when life pushed him down.*

She would want him to be happy, even without her. *And that's what he would want for me...*

Chapter 43

Hannah bundled up the journal, the baby shoes and the gold piece, put them in the velvet bag and then stuffed it all into her big jacket pocket and got herself ready to go out. The wind almost knocked her over when she walked out on the porch, but for some reason it didn't bother her as much as before. She embraced it, faced it and headed for Finis' house down the lane.

Smiley, who had been playing outside, chasing anything that the wind blew, spotted her and fell into place at her side. She looked down at him and he smiled up at her. She reached down and scooped him up and he licked her face.

"You are officially my dog, Smiley! Part of my new family, and nobody will ever take you away from me - I promise!" He seemed to understand her and nuzzled against her neck. Hannah smiled and bundled him up, wrapping her scarf around him. He stayed perfectly still, with only his funny-looking little face poking out into the wind.

Hannah remembered a bumper sticker she had seen once that said, "God, please let me be the person my dog thinks I am." Now she understood how completely dogs loved you, how they thought of their owners as worthy of admiration, loyalty and devotion. She nodded her head and smiled. Dogs had it right. Love someone without reservation, and try to see only their good points. It was a philosophy worthy of imitation.

Finis answered the door, hurrying them inside. "My goodness, Hannah, what in the world brings you out walking in weather like this? - not that I'm not happy to see you! You take off your coat and I'll make us some hot chocolate." He headed off toward the kitchen.

"I found something that I just had to share with you," she answered as she unbundled herself, "and you're not going to believe it!"

He turned to look at her as he puttered around in the kitchen. "Well, don't you sound excited! I have to admit that I am very glad to have the company on a day like this. I was feeling quite landlocked in this house and there's not a face on Hat'tras Island that I'd rather see than yours!"

His words warmed her heart. She went over and threw her arms around him, giving him a big bear hug. "I love you, you big old fierce-looking teddy bear!" she said as she let him go.

Finis stood and looked at her with a confused expression on his face. He hadn't heard those three words in a very long time. His eyes became moist and he turned away, clearing his throat and mindlessly moving things on the counter around. Hannah thought perhaps she had crossed the line with her expression of affection.

Finally, he turned around and looked straight at her. She couldn't read his face; he seemed to be having trouble finding the words, which was a most unusual situation for Finis to find himself in.

"Sit down, Hannah, I'll get the cocoa ready," he said softly, and then turned around and finished up the task. She sat, waiting quietly, until he came to the table with two cups, placing one in front of her and sitting down to his own.

"I...I'm sorry if -" she began

He held up his hand. "Nothing to be sorry about, dear girl. It's just that nobody has said that they... *loved me* in so long that it hit me hard - right here," he said, putting his closed fist over his heart. He cleared his throat. "We had three boys, and Flora and me always wished that we could have had a girl, too. She really wanted a daughter and instead she wound up with a house full of big lugs like me to take care of." He grinned and shook his head.

Hannah smiled and released a breath that she didn't even realize she had been holding.

"So you kinda caught me off guard, you see... But that don't mean that I wasn't glad to hear it, you understand. And the way I feel about you, Hannah, well, it's..." He dropped his chin, searching for words.

She put her hand over his. "It's okay, Finis. You don't have to say anything. I just wanted you to know how dear you are to me, how much having you in my life has come to mean to me..."

The tender look on his face was one that Hannah would never forget. They shared a smile, he squeezed her hand and in that moment no words were needed.

"Oh!" She said. "I completely forgot - the whole reason I came over here was to show you something." She reached over and picked up the old red velvet bag that she'd laid on the table. "Do you recognize this?"

He stared at it, and then took it in his hand, feeling the items inside. "Well, yes and no... let me explain: Granny T told us some tales about a red velvet bag, but for the life of me I can't remember what the stories were... I believe it was tied in with the so-called 'family treasure,' though. But personally, no, I've never seen this bag myself." He handed it back to her.

She began to draw out the items inside, the old baby shoes first, and held them up for him to see.

"That's an old thing if I ever did see one," he said, taking the tiny, worn shoes gently out of her hand and examining them. "I have to wonder how many little babies wore these shoes during their lifetime of service..."

"My thoughts exactly. No doubt they were on the feet of every child in the family. No wonder the mother decided to keep them, all her sweet babies and the memories of them are tied up with those little shoes. And then there's this -" She took out the journal, unwrapped it and handed it to Finis.

He took it from her gently, careful of its age, opened it and spotted the drawing. "What is this? Somebody was a pretty good artist!" He said, touching the old pencil lines. "Wonder who it was?"

She smiled. "I believe it was your great-grandfather, Josiah Miller, the Keeper of the Little Kinnakeet Life Saving Station. But that's the only drawing in there, the rest of it is a personal journal written by - I believe - your great-grandmother. She doesn't mention her own name, but from the way she talks about everyone else, I'm pretty sure that it's hers. What *was* her name, Finis, do you know?"

He shook his head. "No I don't recall, but it's here in the family Bible. He reached over and picked up the large book from a nearby shelf. It had certainly seen its share of wear and tear; small torn slips of papers used as bookmarks stuck out at the top and the tattered leather edges were cracked. Flipping through the pages in the beginning he stopped and said, "Okay, here's the family history. Let's see...that's mamma and daddy, that's Granny T - this was her Bible, by the way. And her parents... Looks like Josiah and Sarah Miller." He looked up at her and smiled.

Hannah grinned from ear to ear. "Sarah. Sarah Miller. Now I have a name to go with the life that I just read about - oh, and Finis, there were pictures in the old chest, I forgot to bring those! I'll bet one of the women in the photos is her! We can actually see what she looked like!" Hannah was so excited that she could hardly sit still.

Finis put down the Bible and picked up the journal again, turning the book over in his hands. "It sure looks old enough. Was there anything interesting in it?" He glanced up at her, a twinkle in his eyes.

She laughed softly. "Only the story of the history of your family... I don't suppose you'd like to read it, would you?"

He laughed and slapped the table. "You bet! But tell me where you found it, where it was hidden. Because I know that if old Midgett had ever found it, it'd be for sale in some antique store or on eBay by now!"

As they drank their cocoa, Hannah told him the story of the old trunk up in the attic and how her boredom had led her to explore its dark corners. He soaked it up like someone thirsty being given a cool drink.

"I don't know what to say..." He handled the old journal gently, giving it the respect it now deserved.

"Don't say anything right now. I want you to read it, and then we can talk about it together. Maybe some of the stories Granny T told you will come back to mind as you read through the entries. Most of it is about your great-grandmother's younger years, but there are also regular entries as she gets older. It's - it's a condensed life, really, Finis, that you're holding in your hands. Your great-grandparents life."

He nodded. "You bet I'll read it. Right now!"

"And on that note, I'm headed home," she said, gathering up the baby shoes and putting them back into the bag. "I'll take this with me and after you've read the journal, we can talk about the incredible story of how Sarah and Josiah met and came to fall in love."

He grinned and waved at her, opening up the journal to the first entry.

"Thanks for the cocoa. See you soon, Finis," she added as she and Smiley opened the door and took their leave. Finis grunted and she knew that he was already engrossed in the same story that she hadn't been able to put down. They made their way home.

Chapter 44

Just as she was taking off her boots (which made her think of the journal entry of how Josiah had brought Sarah some 'real boots'), Smiley began to bark. She peeped out the window and saw Phil's truck pull up in the driveway. He got out, pulled his coat tightly around him and made his way quickly to her door. She opened it before he had a chance to knock.

"Phil! What in the world are you doing out in weather like this? Come in, come in! Take off your coat!"

He grinned at her, flashing that adorable dimple; he took off his coat and sat down. "Well, it's terrible weather out there and I was worried that maybe ...your heater wasn't working, or your pipes might freeze again, or... Well, basically I just wanted to check on you to make sure that you and Smiley were alright." He looked a bit embarrassed.

She gave him her best smile. "Oh, thank you, Phil, that's very kind of you! So far, everything here is fine. I just returned from Finis' house and he's doing well, too, just bored out of his mind like I was. I'm so happy to see you!"

He lit up. "You are? I mean, I sort of invited myself over and I've never been here before, so I wasn't sure..." he said, looking around. "You've fixed this old place up nice."

"Come in and sit down. Can I make you a cup of hot tea?"

He nodded. "...sure, if it's not too much trouble..."

"Not at all. Come on in the kitchen."

He stopped to pet Smiley and talk to him. She watched the two of them together; Smiley obviously loved Phil. *They say animals know who they can trust...maybe I'll be able to figure that out soon, myself.*

He walked into the kitchen. "So, anything interesting happening around here? Everything's all dead in town, hardly anybody out and about."

"Oh, yeah," she said as she made their tea. "I've had quite a day, sit down and let me tell you about it!" She made their tea, sat at the table and shared the story of the findings from her attic with him.

"Can I see that gold coin?" Phil asked after hearing her story.

"Sure," she said, and dug it and the baby shoes out of the red velvet bag. She handed it to him. "It's marked 1868, and I believe it's a twenty-dollar piece..."

He looked at it carefully and smiled. "Sure enough is! What a find! You could sell this for – well, I can Google it and tell you in exactly a minute!" He reached for his phone.

She put her hand on top of his and shook her head. "Not now, Phil. It doesn't matter what it's worth. First of all, I don't need the money; and second, this is the kind of thing that should be a family heirloom. I want Finis to have it, rightfully it's his."

He nodded. "Of course." He looked a little embarrassed.

She grinned. "That was the first thing that popped into my head, too, if it makes you feel any better – that it must be worth a lot of money. But what makes it most precious is not its age or its rarity, but the story behind how Sarah came to have it and what that money meant to her. You'll find all that out when Finis lets you read the journal - and I know he will, when he's done with it."

They sat in silence for several moments, enjoying the warmth of the old kitchen and the comfortable presence of one another.

"Phil, I am so glad that you came today. Right after Finis, you were the next person I wanted to share all of this with. It feels comfortable, 'right', having you sitting at my table. I do hope that you'll come back again, soon."

Taking that as his cue to leave, he stood up. "Hannah, I like you so much that I don't believe I could stay away," he said. "So you'll just have to put up with me coming over and bothering you..." He shrugged.

"If I have to..." She said, winking at him.

Chapter 45

The following morning Finis was knocking on her door before she'd even had her first cup of coffee. She stumbled to the door, saw who it was and opened it. "Finis - it's...early..."

He walked in. "Early, shmerly, it don't matter! I finished the journal and I just had to talk to you about it. Got coffee made?"

She pushed back her messy dark hair, wrapped the belt of her robe tight and shuffled into the kitchen in her furry slippers. "Just made it, come on and have some and help me wake up."

As they sat at the table, Hannah noticed that there was a sparkle in Finis' eyes that she hadn't seen before, and that his smile was bigger and reflected intensely in his eyes. Seeing him this way made her heart happy. Evidently the journal had affected him as it had her.

"So," he said. "I've decided that I want *you* to write a book about my great-grandparents' story." He looked at her as if the idea had been hers, not his.

She blinked her eyes several times and shook her head. "Me, write a book? You're kidding? I'm no writer, Finis, I'm... Well, these days I'm not sure exactly what I am, but outside of a few articles for the college newspaper, I've never written anything that's been published!"

He pointed his finger at her. "See? I knew you were a writer! It's a great story, don't you think? And it's true! I'm sure they'll make a movie out of it like they did that book about the nights in Rodanthe, and that was just a made-up story!"

Hannah laughed. "You overestimate my abilities, my friend. I am flattered by the confidence you have in me, but I've never tried to do anything like that!"

He gave her a fatherly look and lowered his voice. "You do realize, Hannah, that nobody has ever done *anything* until the first time they do it, don't you?" He shrugged. "Oh, and I called Phil and told him to come over here. He should be here soon." He looked at his watch.

"Phil - coming here - now? I've gotta get dressed! You stinker, you should have told me!" She popped up and headed for the bedroom.

"I just did..." he said to her back.

By the time Hannah had made herself presentable, Phil was already at the table having coffee with Finis. *These two feel pretty comfortable here, don't they? Oh, well, I wouldn't have it any other way, I suppose.* She walked into the kitchen. "Make yourself at home, boys!"

"Okay," Phil said. "We're talking about the journal. I brought some donuts over and was just about to make some more coffee if it's alright with you," he said, getting up to greet her.

"Well, that's not my usual breakfast, but this is a special occasion so let's celebrate!" She said, smiling at him.

"Special occasion?" Finis asked.

"Yes," she said, moving over and putting her hand on the older man's shoulder. "It is my honor today to give you a valuable piece of your family history!" She looked at Phil and smiled; he sat back down.

Finis squinted at her. "I thought you did that yesterday..."

She shook her head and sat at the table. "Well, yes, but not all of it. I was saving something special for after you had finished reading the journal. You did finish it, didn't you?"

"Oh, yes! And I dug out some old family letters and documents and used them and the family Bible to fill in a few more facts. That's what I wanted to tell you about. Turns out that Sarah had her own little sewing business and made clothes for people on the island. And later, she and Josiah built a school! But what is this valuable piece of family history you're talking about?"

She smiled and reached deep inside the red velvet bag. "It's a twenty-dollar gold piece dated 1868, and I believe that it's the last of the money Sarah inherited from the family she traveled with. Now it's yours!" She handed it to him.

He took it, studied it and turned it over and over in his fingers. "A piece of their life. A piece of my history. It really is real..." He stared at it and then looked up with tears in his eyes. "Oh, Hannah, thank you - thank you for everything!" He wiped his eyes with the back of his hand. "Sorry, I'm gettin' all emotional on ya'll here - that's not like me!"

"We know it's not, Finis," Phil said, winking at Hannah. "Not at all."

"It's yours to keep, Finis. As far as I'm concerned, it's your inheritance," Hannah said.

Finis looked up. "But there's other survivin' family members around. I do have some cousins, like old Midgett. Rightfully, part of it belongs to them, I suppose..."

Hannah shook her head. "Well, if whatever washes up on the beach belongs to whoever finds it, then I believe that whatever turns up in *my* attic belongs to *me*. And I am giving that gold coin to *you*. So those cousins don't even figure into it and never have to know anything about it!"

Finis grinned. "Never argue with a woman!"

Phil nodded. "Especially when she's right!"

Finis gave him a look of pity. "They're always right, you idiot, don't you know that?"

Chapter 46

Hannah drove north toward Avon, Smiley sitting shotgun. His stubby little tail wagged furiously as they passed flocks of seagulls. Soon the windsurfers would be out, and the waters of the Pamlico Sound would be filled with the color of their sails. The roads and stores would be jammed with tourists, money would flow into the pockets of the local economy and life would be good here on the Outer Banks.

'Life on a sandbar,' like the bumper stickers said. Hannah smiled as she thought about it.

When Phil had asked her to come to work for him part-time, she wasn't sure about it, but she'd come to love working with the animals, both large and small. He had taught her so much, and allowed Smiley to come to work with her. The work had been just what she needed.

The letter she had written to the teenage driver who had killed her husband – well, it was difficult, but she knew that to move forward she would have to forgive the girl. No doubt embarrassment had kept the girl from writing back, but to Hannah that really didn't matter. The forgiveness in her own heart was the important thing, and that had come finally.

And the book she was writing - well, it would be quite a while before it was finished, but she was finding that perhaps she might be a writer after all. The local research she was doing had drawn her even closer to life on Hatteras Island; she now felt that she was a part of this special place.

Leaving Columbus last year, Hannah had been hurting, confused and unsure about even wanting to go on. But now she knew – for sure – that going on, not giving up on life or on people – it had been the right thing to do, the best decision she could have made.

Phil was funny, intelligent and always doing something that took her by surprise. She smiled, thinking of how he had bumped into her at work the other day, apologized, and then spun her around and kissed her good and proper right there in front of everybody. Smiley had yipped, bounced up and down and then everybody went back to business as usual.

He had given her all the space she needed to grieve, to remember Mark, and to discover who she was as a person without the man she had built her old life around. Like any serious wound, hers had needed time to heal – from the inside out.

Now Hannah knew that it was time to move forward, time to remember Mark for the amazing man that he had been. She would treasure every memory and go forward to make new ones with a man who also understood her, and yes, even loved her. She thought of him, his love for animals and people, his devotion to their friend Finis – so many things to admire about the man. Totally different from her first innocent love, this love was a mature one.

Her shift at the clinic today started after lunch, and as she pulled into the parking lot, she noticed a large handwritten sign on the locked door of the veterinary clinic. It said,

'HANNAH - EMERGENCY AT CHICAMACOMICO - NEED YOUR HELP - HURRY, PHIL'

She and Smiley jumped back into the car and headed north. *What kind of emergency could this be? Especially at a museum?* Granted, Chicamacomico was a living museum, and the people who ran it did their best to preserve the history of the Life Saving Service, but did they even *have* any animals on the property?

In the old days, Life Saving Stations had kept draft horses on the property to pull the heavy beach apparatus through the sand, but Hannah didn't remember seeing any kind of animals currently at Chicamacomico. She shook her head. Who knows? Maybe the animal belonged to one of the museum workers... No sense trying to figure it out, she'd be there soon enough. This was an odd thing, though, even on an island full of oddities.

Chapter 47

She parked in the crowded lot, and ran up to the Station. The Station Manager met her outside, waved his arms and pointed her toward the beach, over the dunes. Hannah and Smiley took off running.

As they crested the top of the dunes, she noticed that the crew had set up the Beach Apparatus Drill. Once a week during the summer months, local Coast Guard volunteers re-enacted the procedure the old Life Savers had gone through, setting up the cannon-fired lines and the breeches buoy, performing a mock rescue. It was a sight to see, and truly gave observers the feel of what it must have been like to be a part of it all those years ago.

It looked to Hannah like the men were coming to the end of the demonstration, to the delight of a large group of tourists. She looked around for Phil, but didn't see him anywhere. The Coast Guard volunteers looked busy with their work, and she didn't want to bother them, so she waited. *It was all very confusing... Had she read the note on the office door wrong?*

Hannah heard the loud applause as the drill re-enactment came to an end. Suddenly, the Station Site Manager was there, asking for everyone's attention.

"Normally, this would conclude our drill," he said, smiling. "But today we have a special treat for all of you." He turned and motioned, and Phil came up to stand beside him. "This is our local veterinarian, Phil Crawford. He's a stand-up guy, a great vet and a valuable member of our community. He has a special announcement that he wants to make today." He turned toward Phil and handed him the microphone.

Phil locked eyes with Hannah and smiled. "Hannah, could you please join me up here?" She looked around for a reason and didn't see one. "Folks, would you please get Hannah Stewart up here for me?" He pointed her out; the crowd applauded and she moved in a daze toward Phil, who took her hand.

He grinned, that dimple flashing. "Hannah is my assistant at the veterinary clinic. She's been living on Hat'tras Island for over a year now. She's from Ohio, but nobody around here holds that against her." There was general laughter. A few shouts were heard from the crowd, "Ohio! Yeah!"

Phil went on. "My friends here at Chicamacomico agreed to help me out with a special project today. Over a hundred twenty-five years ago, a girl washed up on this beach – she was the sole survivor of a terrible shipwreck. She was recused by the brave surfmen who manned the Little Kinnakeet Station, down the road. That woman, Sarah Miller, wound up marrying the surfman who rescued her and living the rest of her life here. She became the great-grandmother of a dear friend of mine, Finis Turnbull." He pointed toward the crowd. "Take a bow, Finis!"

Finis moved to the front, rolled his eyes and took a dramatic bow for the crowd. They cheered him eagerly.

Phil said, "Finis is a native and lifelong resident of the Outer Banks, and if you want to know anything about our local history, ask him. Because he knows everything about everything and has plenty of time to tell you about it!" The crowd laughed again. Finis gave Phil a look.

Hannah was feeling quite uncomfortable; after all, he'd called her here for an emergency, and this felt like some kind of a set-up. What was he doing?

Phil turned to her and smiled. "But back to the special project. Living on this island - or anywhere, for that matter - is made so much better by having the people we love around us. And I fell in love with this woman the moment I laid eyes on her, when she brought a pitiful, scraggly little abandoned dog in to me." He looked down at Smiley, petted him, and the little dog jumped waist high.

The crowd *awwww-ed*.

"Because our life is here and tied up with the local history in many ways, I wanted to make this a special occasion. So I asked my friends here at Chicamacomico Station to help me out." He turned to Hannah, took her hand and got down on one knee. He reached in his pocket and took out a ring.

"Hannah Stewart, you beautiful, sweet, incredible woman, would you please make my life complete, and marry me?"

The crowd went wild.

Hannah went stiff. *In front of all these people! He just asked me to marry him on the beach in front of all these people!*

When no answer was immediately forthcoming, Phil began to get a little nervous and whispered, "Hannah, did you hear me?" The crowd had hushed, waiting for her answer.

She shook herself out of her shock. "I did - I mean - I do - I mean I will!"

He stood up, slipped the ring on her finger and took her in his arms, kissing her the way that he had always wanted to kiss her. The kiss went on for so long that the Site Manager took the microphone out of Phil's hand, cleared his throat and said, "Let's hear it for the newly engaged couple, folks!" Then he added, "And, yes we do weddings here at the Station if you know anyone who's interested!"

The crowd yelled, clapped and hooted, which finally brought Phil and Hannah back to consciousness. They turned, waved to the crowd. Hannah was beet-red, but smiling from ear to ear. Everyone offered them congratulations and the crowd wandered off. Finis was left standing there, and he walked up to them. "About time, you two!" He said, giving Hannah and Phil both a bear hug. "About time!"

Hannah was so happy that she was near tears. "Thank you, Finis. And, if we're getting married…"

"We are!" Phil interrupted.

She smiled at him. "Yes, I mean *when* we get married, would you be the one to give away the bride, please?"

The old man choked up. For the longest time, he couldn't say anything. Finally, he just nodded. "Uh-huh," was all he could get out. She hugged him again and whispered, "thank you" in his ear. He squeezed her so tight that she almost couldn't take a breath.

He finally let her go and said to them, "I have an engagement present for the two of you. And I don't want to hear an argument about it from either one of you, you understand?" He gave them his best stink-eye.

They nodded and laughed. He handed them a small box, wrapped in silver paper. Hannah took it, looked up at him and said, "This is so thoughtful of you, Finis..."

He grunted. "Well, open it already!"

She smiled and tore off the paper. She folded back the tissue paper inside and there inside was – the 1868 twenty-dollar gold piece!

Hannah shook her head vigorously. "No, no, Finis, this belongs in your family! We can't take this! No way!"

Phil chimed in, "Finis, this is too much..."

He put his hands on his hips and stared at them. "I told you both - no arguments! This will stay *in my family*, because you two are part of my family, don't you know that? And when you have a house full of younguns, you can give it to one of them and they can pass it down to one of their younguns. That way, it will stay *in our family* for generations. You just have to promise to tell them all about the story behind it.". He pointed his finger at them. "Oh, and also about their wonderful Uncle Finis - be sure to remember that part!"

Hannah began to cry. The emotional tension she had been feeling started to pour out and she boo-hoo'd for several minutes.

Phil and Finis just stared at each other, shaking their heads.

Phil asked, "Do women always cry when they're happy, Finis?"

He shook his head. "You got a lot to learn, boy! No, they don't! And sometimes when they cry, it means they're very *unhappy*! And you have to learn to tell the difference!"

"How long does *that* take?" Phil asked, swallowing hard.

"Oh, forty or fifty years ought to do it..."

Phil got a scared, stupid look on his face, which caused Finis and Hannah to laugh and hug each other even tighter.

THE END

Thank you so very much for reading my novel! As an independent author of 'clean books', I am supported by readers like you, who enjoy being entertained by a good story told without gratuitous sex and violence.

Please – please – take a moment and go to *amazon.com* to leave a brief review of the book. Thank you so much for doing that! I appreciate all my readers and am very grateful to you for taking the time to read and share my stories!

Sharron Frink

Feel free to contact me through my website:

sharronfrink.com

Little Kinnakeet Life Saving Station was an actual, working Life Saving Station near Rodanthe, North Carolina. Designed by Francis Ward Chandler, Little Kinnakeet was built in 1874 in the Gothic/Stick style. In 1905 it was replaced with a larger, Southern style building, and the old station was used as a boathouse.

original 1874 Station

newer 1905 station

(photos courtesy of National Park Service)

The fictional characters in this book never existed; they are, as we say in the South, "made-up" people. So any similarity to persons living or dead is purely coincidental and definitely not intended.

However, the actual surfmen who worked these stations from 1874 until they were closed in 1954 (when the stations were decommissioned and made part of the National Park Service) were real, brave, selfless men. The record of their efforts is clear and documented.

In the forty-four-year history of the U.S. Life-Saving Service, 177,286 lives were saved of the 178,741 lives in peril (99.2%), a record unparalleled even today. At the same time and due to their unrivaled training, less than one percent loss of life was recorded for the actual U.S. Life Saver surfmen themselves.

The original Keeper of Little Kinnakeet, Banister Midgett, was appointed on Dec. 4, 1874. He left the service in 1876. After him, L.B. Midgett, John A. Midgett, Edward O. Hooper, Edward S. Midgett and Baxter B. Miller (a Gold Life Saving Medal Recipient) all served as the Keepers of Little Kinnakeet.

Both the old station and the newer one are in the process of being restored. The site is located north of Avon on the west side of NC 12, 2/10-mile north of mile marker 52. look for a dirt road on the sound side. It's an unmarked location, but you may see the tower. Currently, it is behind a chain-link fence and not open to the public, but you can drive up and take a look from outside the fence.

The restoration is in progress, but it has had setbacks in recent years. Please support this project and also come and visit the remaining station, Chicamacomico, which is an excellent restored museum of the activities of these brave men. If you come in the summer months, you can also watch a re-enactment of the Breeches Buoy rescue by Coast Guard volunteers.

93800530R00126

Made in the USA
Columbia, SC
23 April 2018